MOLLY HALLELUJAH!

Selkirk Stories™ and the image of a heart with three
stars are trademarks of Selkirk Stories, Cornwall,
Prince Edward Island, Canada.

MOLLY HALLELUJAH!

by

MARGARET A. WESTLIE

Selkirk
STORIES

Chapter 1

"This meeting will come to order!" Molly, a spirit of some repute, rapped her oaken gavel on the top of the tombstone. The evening shadows swirled and settled as the company of spirits gave Molly their attention. Molly had already proven her worth as a psychic from the earthly side of things, and had been building on her reputation as an irascible, prickly spirit who knew how to get things done. She had recently been given the assignment of overseeing new spirits as they learned their place on that side of the veil.

"You know that there's trouble brewing at the church here." Molly gestured with the gavel toward the church by the graveyard.

Betty Lou sniffed. "If there isn't, there should be." She sniffed again. "It was getting bad enough a few months ago when I was still there." Betty Lou had been a long time member of the church in question and had been quite outspoken on its flaws since she had come over and almost as much as when she was still there.

Everyone nodded. A miscellany of "Amens" and "Say it again, sister," floated on the crisp fall air. The leaves rustled and the odour of damp vegetation wafted from around the tombstones.

Lucy, in her buttoned down twin set, sat on a flat tombstone to the left of Molly, taking notes. She swung her feet in their penny loafers with the new copper gleaming in the slot. She and Molly had been best friends in their earthly lives and the friendship had continued when Molly had made her transition shortly after Lucy's own.

"I think it's nearly time for us to take a hand in the situation before the church is completely ruined." Molly gestured toward the church in question with the handle of her gavel. "I would like to appoint a steering committee for this operation. I thought perhaps with me at the head and Lucy to take notes I'd only need one other person."

While Molly paused for breath Lucy tried to intervene. She was a gentle soul and her mission was to keep Molly in check as best she could. "Now Molly, you know we can't interfere with the people on the other side. It's up to them to run their own affairs"

"Nonsense," said Molly, "they can't handle their own affairs. They need our help, and a little tweak here and a tiny nudge there certainly can't hurt."

Molly ignored Lucy and returned her attention to the business at hand. "I think Betty Lou is a good candidate since she has just come over and will have first hand knowledge of the problems involved." Betty Lou Ettinger had sung in the choir and taught Sunday School at various times in her sojourn at the church.

There was a general nodding of heads and a few whispers among the assembly.

"Libby, you were good friends with the pastor's mother while you were over there."

"Yes, but that was a long time ago." Libby pulled her cardigan closer around her shoulders. "I didn't have much influence with her then. I'll have even less now."

Molly nodded. "You keep close contact with her son, don't you?"

Libby nodded, then sneezed. "He was not much influence then either. He was one of the most henpecked men I've ever known." She rummaged in her pocket for a tissue. "I was talking to him just yesterday and he's still apologizing for his behaviour, though I have yet to figure out what he's talking about." She scrubbed at her nose with the tissue, then sniffed."I'll talk to him again. This may be the opportunity he's been waiting for all his life."

Molly chuckled. "It may indeed." She leaned over, pulled her stockings up and refastened the knot that held them above her knees. "I only need one more."

Lucy tapped Molly's forearm with the end of her pencil. "What about Larry?"

"Oh, Larry! He's too busy, so he says. But you can bet your bottom dollar he'll be doing the heavy looking on when we least need him." Molly floated to the top of her tombstone and sat tapping the gavel into the palm of her left hand.

"He can act as consultant," said Lucy, "and he is our boss after all. It doesn't seem right not to involve him."

Molly made a face. "Humph! I guess you're right, but he's usually a wet blanket." She paused and thought for a moment. "So I still need one other member on this committee." She transferred the gavel to her left hand and began tapping it into the palm of her right hand.

Lucy leaned over and took the gavel from Molly's hand and laid it on the tombstone between them. "You'll hurt yourself." She went back to taking notes.

"What about Meredith?" said Libby. "She's just recently come over and she became a good friend of Mrs. Waters after I left."

A chorus of noes filled the darkening air. Christie's voice came through over the babble. "Meredith hasn't much backbone and she still hasn't made up her mind if she's staying here this time."

"She'd better make it up soon," said Molly, "or they'll be taking her off to the undertaker before she has a chance to get back. She has been in and out of coma for the last six weeks." Molly scratched her hairy chin. "But you know, you may be onto something. We can persuade her to go back and be an interpreter for us." Molly's eyes sparkled. "Yes, I think that's what we'll do."

"Where is she now?" asked Lucy.

"Still at Sunrise Manor, I think," said Libby. "She hasn't recovered enough to be discharged yet. I can drop in and see her this evening and find out what she's thinking. The last time I talked to her she was terribly depressed and wouldn't even get out of bed."

"Maybe this will be just what she needs, said Molly. "If she liked the earthly side of things so much maybe she'll be glad of the chance to return even in spirit form. I don't know her well enough to say."

"Do thomething with these, Mith Alberta." Pastor Waters handed his secretary an untidy handful of papers with one hand and stifled a hiccup with the other.

Alberta took the stack and thumped the papers into

neatness on the edge of the dictionary which lay open in front of her. She leafed through the first several pages to discover their topic. The notes of yesterday's sermon were wrinkled, ringed and spotted. She chose not to inspect them further nor to identify the spots.

Pastor Waters suppressed another hiccup. "That'th my good girl. I know I can depend on you." He turned and wandered away down the hall.

Alberta stared after him, raising a bushy grey eyebrow when he bumped into the door frame to his office, then disappeared inside. She turned to the filing cabinet and began fingering her way through sermon files for the topic nearest to the sermon in hand. "Bible, humility, parenting." She muttered her way through to gambling and dropped the latest contribution to posterity into the holding file.

"Good morning, Alberta." Jane Ridgeway balanced a large carton on one knee and the edge of Alberta's desk. "What shall I do with these? They belong to Sam. He held choir practice at Sandra Hughes' last evening.

He walked home and asked me if I would get this box of music back here."

Alberta walked around the desk to relieve Jane of her burden. "How is Sandra these days? She has had a terrible siege with her heart failure this time."

"She seems well, though a little weak." Jane shook her arms to restore circulation. "She only sang for part of the rehearsal."

"It was kind of Sam to have rehearsal at her house. She does love to sing." Alberta turned toward Sam's office. "Open the door for me, please."

Jane rapped on the door, then opened it. "Good morning, Sam." She held the door wide for Alberta. "I'm just returning your music."

Pastor Sam jumped to his feet and took the box from Alberta. "Thank you so much, I really appreciate you doing this." Sam stood smiling down at Jane.

Alberta caught the warm glow in Sam's brown eyes then averted her gaze. So that's the way it is, she thought. She glanced at Jane who did not seem to notice anything. I'll just watch and see what comes of this, she thought, then turned back to her desk.

Presently Jane returned to the outer office and sat down in one of the straight chairs and crossed her knees. "So how's the world treating you, Alberta?"

"Well enough, I suppose. It's always busy here this time of year, what with Christmas pageant auditions starting this week." She laced her hands behind her head and stretched her shoulders. "I suppose there'll be umpteen changes in the script before they're done."

Jane laughed. It was a pleasant sound. "And every one will require a new typing."

"You got it." Alberta pursed her lips, the fine grey moustache that covered her upper lip wrinkled and bunched. "I've never seen such a production before Jarrod came on staff, and never a word of thanks."

"He is kind of full of himself, isn't he." Jane picked up a pencil and began turning it end for end on Alberta's desk.

Alberta gave a small snort. "He's not the only one."

"Why do you put up with it?" Jane thumped the pencil on the desk too hard and broke the lead.

"I've been here since the church started thirty years ago. I know everyone and as much of their troubles as they care to tell me." Alberta took the pencil from Jane and stuck it in the electric sharpener. "And it is my bread and butter." The pencil sharpener ground to a stop. Alberta returned the pencil to the jar on the front of her desk then moved the jar out of Jane's reach.

"You've been here all my life."

"And most of my own." Alberta sighed.

"You must have started from high school."

"Right from secretarial school. I've known all the pastors who have ever worked here. I remember when they first talked about hiring an associate pastor, and now they have two, Sam and Jarrod."

"Good morning, Miss Alberta." The office door banged against the wall. "I've proofread these scripts, and they're full of typos." Jarrod's pink eyelashes fluttered over pale blue eyes. He dropped the stack of manuscripts he was carrying onto the middle of Alberta's desk. The gust of air created scattered the letters that Alberta had been working on everywhere.

"I'll let you pick those up, you'll know what order they were in better than I do." His freckled face wrinkled into an expression somewhere between a grimace and a smile. "By the way, I want those typos corrected by tomorrow morning. I want to proofread them again." He turned to leave. "Oh, and by the way, Jim Randle will be coming by about two this afternoon. We're lucky to have such fine carpenter in our congregation. I want a pot of fresh coffee and some real cream for then." He opened the door more quietly than before, the fluorescent lighting made the bald patch on the crown of his head gleam. The door slammed behind him.

Jane made a face. "I see what you mean." She watched Jarrod's thin form disappear into the shadows of the darkened hallway. "I wouldn't put up with that from him. That's just plain rude and egotistical." She picked up one of the scripts. "May I?"

Alberta shrugged. "Go ahead. They're probably practically illegible anyway. I don't understand why he doesn't proofread them before I make two dozen copies."

"Maybe he fancies himself a big playwright from Toronto." Jane chuckled and began leafing through the pages.

"Gosh! He's got corrections in every paragraph."

"Yes, and there's likely at least three pages that I've never seen before."

Jane set the script back on the pile and stood up. "Well, I'm sorry he does that to you. You'll be busy all day with it, so I'd better go and let you get at it. I have a class to teach in forty-five minutes anyway, and I left my briefcase at home so I'll have to get that. Toodle-oo." She left, closing the office door quietly behind herself.

Alberta bent herself to the task of deciphering Jarrod's notes and misinterpretations. *I wonder if I just retyped these would he notice.* She curled her lip slightly at the thought. *I'll try a page later on and just see if he does.* She typed the letters of the manuscript into her computer. This doesn't even resemble what he had before. She shook her head and stuck her pencil more firmly behind her ear. She worked her way through the altered play. By noon she was half done. She looked up from her work and stretched her arms behind her head. The outside door opened and she put her arms down and straightened her jacket. The office door swung slightly in the gust of cold air.

"Hi, Alberta." Maggie Morley leaned against the office door to shut it against the cold autumn wind that had followed her inside.

"Maggie! I wasn't expecting you until tomorrow." Alberta turned from her computer and leaned her elbows on the desk.

Maggie opened her coat and collapsed onto the nearest chair. "I know." She bunched up her lower lip. "I have a problem. Pastor Jarrod wanted me to buy material for the costumes for the pageant. I've been to every fabric store here and in Summerside. They're all out of gold and silver lame. The high school drill teams are going to nationals the first week in January just before school starts again and they got there ahead of me." She sighed and stared at her feet. The snow in the treads of her boots was slowly melting into a puddle around her feet. "I'm beat." She sat up straight and tucked her feet under her chair to hide the melt water. "I don't know what I'm going to do."

Alberta clucked her tongue in sympathy. "I guess you'll have to tell Pastor Jarrod the situation." She clucked her tongue again. "I don't envy you the job."

Maggie looked over at her. "What kind of mood is he in these days?"

"He's just starting to wind up for pageant. I'm only on my second revision of the script."

"Is he in?"

Alberta nodded.

Maggie slid out of her chair and stood up. "I guess I'd better go and see him."

"Good luck." Rather you than me, thought Alberta. She turned toward her work.

After a few moments the sound of a door slamming and raised voices disturbed her concentration. She frowned and listened more intently to the voices. It was mainly Jarrod who was speaking. He's being sarcastic, thought Alberta. It's bad news when he sounds sarcastic. After a few minutes the voices ceased and Maggie came into the office. Her usually tidy hair was ruffled and her face was flushed. She looked to be on the verge of tears.

Alberta turned away from her work and handed Maggie a box of tissues and Maggie waved them away.

"Whatever happened in there?" Alberta set the box of tissues within Maggie's reach.

"He called me names." Maggie shut her jaws with a snap.

"What did he say about the cloth?"

"He said he didn't care how I got it. I was to get it even if I had to go to New York."

"New York's a long way. I don't suppose he offered to pay your way?"

Maggie produced a tiny giggle, then sniffed. "Of course not. I suppose I'd better go a little farther afield. I just hope I can find some."

"D'you mean you're going to try harder for him?" Alberta looked hard at Maggie.

Maggie shrugged. "It's no worse than you typing his script fifteen times. And he knows my time is my own."

Alberta nodded. "You're right." She sighed then pushed her chair back against the wall. "Let's go to lunch."

Alberta lay in bed trying to read herself to sleep that evening but thoughts of her conversation with Maggie kept getting in the way. They had gone to the Eager Beaver diner out on the highway. It was their day for liver and onions, and both she and Maggie liked how the cook fixed it.

"I don't see how you do it, year after year," said Maggie. She pulled the plastic off a package of crackers and bit into one.

"Do what?" Alberta smoothed the red checked oil-cloth with her hands.

"Work for him every day all day for it seems like forever." She tore into another package of crackers.

"It does seem like forever since he came to work here." Alberta brushed some of Maggie's scattered crumbs aside. "But it has only been five years." She watched Maggie destroy another package of crackers. "I'm retiring next year. I keep reminding myself of it."

"I don't know how you do it."

"He's usually not so hard on me. He needs my services. Besides, he wants to progress to Senior Pastor when Mr. Waters retires."

"Is he retiring?"

"He should." Alberta clamped her lips shut.

Chapter 2

Molly and Lucy sat on the front steps of the church passing the time of day. Lucy pulled her new blue twin set more closely around her shoulders. "It sure is cold these days."

"It's late fall," replied Molly. "You should have worn your coat."

"I gave it away," said Lucy, "and I haven't had a chance to make another one. It takes me almost two days of total concentration to manifest anything as complicated as a coat."

Molly frowned. "You were always too generous. Who'd you give it to this time?"

Lucy began to shiver. "I gave it to an old lady down at the warehouse last week. She had none and it was a cold day."

Molly shook her head and shrugged. "I suppose she was a worthy recipient. How'd you get it to her?"

"I manifested it to her. She was sitting by the back

door wishing for a warm place to go, and I just put it around her shoulders."

Molly opened her coat and held it so that Lucy could snuggle in. "I hope she thanked you."

"I think she was too startled to think of it. She would be dead by now if I hadn't done it." Lucy's shiver reduced itself to a fine tremor. "She strayed away from the nursing home in September. Her son is frantic with worry."

"I suppose they don't know if she's dead or alive."

Lucy settled more closely against the faint warmth of Molly's skinny frame. "The police have given up. They expect to find her dead under an overpass someday. Of course, her son is still looking."

"He's the devoted type, is he?"

Lucy nodded. "He's a good man. He has a kind wife, too."

Molly scratched her hairy chin. "Maybe we should put him on the right track to find his mother."

"I already did," said Lucy. "He should find her tomorrow late in the afternoon."

"You were always so kind and thoughtful," said Molly. "A much nicer person than I ever was."

Lucy stood up. "Now, Molly, don't talk about yourself like that. You give people some real practical help when they need it." She began buttoning her cardigan. "Why, look at what you're doing to help the ladies in the church."

"That's nothing," Molly shrugged her left shoulder. "I just give them a push in the right direction when they need it."

"But you carry a task to its appropriate end."

"So do you."

Lucy sat down on the step again. "I just do spot jobs. I can never see the big picture."

Molly patted Lucy's arm. "Sometimes spot jobs are all that's needed." She subsided into silence and stared out across the graveyard. Presently she said: "If we're going to get this church job done before Christmas, we're going to have to stir our stumps."

Lucy nodded. "I want to be home before that."

Molly floated up. "This is vacation, but it has to end sometime." She cleared her throat. "I want Christmas to look like Christmas at least."

Lucy sat looking up at Molly. "Do you have anything in mind yet?"

Molly nodded. "I had lunch with Miss Alberta and her friend yesterday. I encouraged the two of them to talk to the waitress. She had a lot to say about unions and strikes and grievances."

Lucy chuckled. "How much of what she said can you lay claim to?"

"Most of it." Molly pursed her lips making the mole with all the grey whiskers stand up. "We can let this percolate for a few days."

Lucy coughed into her handkerchief then pulled her sweater more closely around her shoulders.

"I can see I'm going to have to manifest you a coat right away before you catch your death of pneumonia."

Lucy stood up. "As if I could anymore. In any case, I can manifest a coat for myself."

Molly stared at Lucy and presently a new blue coat wrapped itself around Lucy's shoulders. "I can do it faster," said Molly.

"I didn't realize that it would be so cold at this time of year," said Lucy. "I'd have brought my long johns and some trousers."

Molly laughed a short harsh laugh. "As if you ever wear anything except twin sets and skirts."

Alberta picked up the telephone after the first ring.

"Church of Saint Bridget. May I help you?"

"Alberta, this is Maggie. I was talking to a couple of the ladies this morning. They're about as fed up as we are. They're ready to do whatever it takes to solve the situation." Maggie paused for breath.

"I see. You do realize that I'm the only one who stands to lose her livelihood."

"I know. That's why we're going to let you work from behind the scenes. We need your help too much to totally exclude you, but we don't want to get you in trouble either."

"That's thoughtful," said Alberta. "Just how do you plan to accomplish that?"

"We haven't gotten that far yet, but we're having a meeting tonight at Lizzie's to see what we need to do."

"Have you included old Mrs. Waters?"

"Are you kidding? Of course not. She'll be the last to know and maybe not even then." Maggie took a deep breath. "So you'll come?"

"I'll be there." Alberta set the phone into its cradle just as the office door opened. She jumped to her feet and went to hold it open for Mrs. Waters. "Aggie! How nice to see you."

Mrs. Waters, plump and bent nearly double with osteoporosis, struggled into the church office. She used the crook of her cane to draw one of the chairs closer then sat down in it with a thump. Tipping her head back to look at Alberta she said: "And where might you be going?"

"To a friend's house." Alberta kept her face still and

stared back at Mrs. Waters.

"Someone from church?"

Alberta cleared her throat. "No one you'd know." She cleared her throat again. "What can I do for you today?"

"I think you're lying to me." Mrs. Waters thumped her cane on the floor. "If you are I'll have your job. Is Teddy in his office?"

"He was a few minutes ago, and I haven't seen him leave." Alberta cleared her throat again.

Mrs. Waters heaved herself to her feet. She balanced herself with the aid of her cane and looked Alberta as much in the eye as she could from her bent position. "You'd better do something about that cold of yours before it gets any worse. This is one of the busiest seasons of the year and we need every pair of hands we can get." She turned toward her son's office.

Alberta shook her head. It's not a cold, she thought. And I am lying. I never thought I'd stoop so low. She settled herself behind her desk and began typing on the manuscript where she had left off.

Presently Aggie Waters returned with Teddy in tow.

"Teddy has a migraine. He's taking the rest of the day off." She hitched herself toward the door with her cane. "Come along Teddy. A hot toddy's what you need."

Pastor Waters stepped around his mother to hold the door for her. "I'm coming, Mother." He hiccuped behind his hand. "Good day, Mith Alberta."

Alberta knocked on Lizzie's front door then let herself in. She dusted off her shoes on the door mat then followed the sound of voices to the kitchen. Molly floated behind her, unnoticed by anyone.

"Good evening, everyone." Alberta set a tray of cookies on the table and peeled out of her winter coat. "Has the meeting started already?" She stuffed her scarf into her left coat sleeve and hung them on the coat rack by the back door.

Maggie peeked under the dish towel that covered the tray. "Yum! Chocolate chip, my favourite!"

"You shouldn't have, Alberta." said Lizzie. "It's such

a lot of trouble."

Alberta shrugged. "The only trouble I took was a trip to the bakery and I was going past anyway." She perched herself on a stool by the breakfast bar. "I figured we'd need some sustenance before we got through this evening."

"Coffee for everyone?" asked Lizzie.

Alberta nodded and sighed, pulling into herself the warm and happy atmosphere of Lizzie's kitchen. "Your geraniums are doing well, Lizzie."

Lizzie tweaked a dying leaf on one of the red ones. "I've always had good luck growing geraniums. These were my mother's you know. I've managed to keep them going for fifteen years." She returned to her task of filling the coffee pot. "If you ever want a start you may certainly have one." She began counting scoops of coffee into the basket. "It does them a world of good to be pinched back now and again." She plugged the coffee pot in, then turned to the group of women gathered around her kitchen table. "I think we're all here now.

Who's going to chair this meeting?"

For a moment no one spoke. Then Maggie Morley said: "I guess it's me since it was my bright idea." She pulled her notebook towards herself, opened it and began taking roll call.

"I think this first meeting should be an assessment meeting. We need to identify the parameters of our problem." She wrote "problem" onto her notebook then lifted her head to look at each woman in turn. "It'll help us understand if we even have a problem.

"We have a problem," said Jane. "In fact, we have several problems." She picked up a napkin and began folding it into a fan. "The first one's name is Jarrod, and the second one's name is Teddy." She unfolded her napkin. "I don't know which one's the worst."

"Teddy's not hard to manage," offered Alberta. "It's Jarrod who needs correction." She lifted the cloth off the tray of cookies.

"What I don't understand," said Jane, "is how Teddy manages to prepare and preach a sermon every week."

Alberta pursed her lips. "I have a suspicion that Aggie does most of it for him. I don't think he has the organization or the depth to create as eloquently as he seems to do every week."

Sandra's laugh was wheezy. Cold weather always caused her asthma to flare. "He's always had such a lisp but it completely disappears when he's in the pulpit. I know when we were in grade school the kids used to tease him terribly."

"That is a strange thing," said Maggie. "Now that you mention it, I remember being very surprised when he went into the ministry."

The ladies fell silent. In the background the coffee pot gurgled and hissed. Maggie took a deep breath. "We've got to stay on track. What problems can we identify originating with the pastors?" She poised her pencil over her notebook.

"Disrespect, I think, is the main one," said Alberta. "Everything else ties into it one way or the other."

Lizzie began pouring coffee. "I think it's a disgrace

the way they take Alberta for granted. She's the one who holds the place together."

"Thank you for saying so," said Alberta. "I've been hanging on by the skin of my teeth waiting for retirement."

"Aren't all the Sunday school teachers women?" asked Sandra. "And isn't Jarrod in charge of that too?"

Alberta nodded. "Unfortunately. We haven't had a peaceful Sunday school department since he took it over." She stirred her coffee, took a sip, then added more sugar.

"I think we need to brainstorm what our options are," said Maggie.

Molly clapped silently from her perch on top of the fridge. "Go for it, Maggie."

"Amen!" said Lucy.

Molly chuckled. "You're beginning to sound like them."

"I've always absorbed my surroundings," said Lucy. "Shush and listen."

"I've been thinking that we should go on strike." Maggie firmed her lips and nodded. "I've been giving it a lot of thought and I think that's our best option."

"Go on strike?" The women's voices sounded as one.

"How can we do that?" asked Sandra. "We have no leverage."

"Of course, we do." Jane's answer silenced the group. "Look, we know already that we do most of the work around there. The place would collapse without us. We've just got to impress that upon the pastorate, and striking will have the most clout."

Lizzie passed the tray of cookies. "How are we going to convince all the ladies of this need? And what are we going to do about Aggie?"

Maggie waved Aggie away with her hand. "We'll just keep her in the dark. I know we can do it. Look at the time that Pastor Waters ditched the car. That didn't come out for a long time and when anyone asked, no one knew anything about it."

"Can we keep that kind of secret?" asked Sandra.

"After all, we're a gossipy bunch." She picked a chocolate chip out of her cookie and popped it into her mouth.

"We'll have nothing to gossip about." Maggie took a sip of her coffee. "We'll all be in it together."

"I think it's a great idea," said Jane. "This is just the time to do it. We'll kill two birds with one stone."

"Who's the other bird?" Sandra's eyes widened.

"If we go on strike at just the right moment we'll get Jarrod too," said Jane, "and of all the pastorate, he needs to be 'got' the worst."

"The Christmas pageant is the ideal time," said Alberta. "We'll play along as if everything is like it always is and at the last moment we'll just not show up."

"What about you?" asked Sandra.

"I have nothing to do with it." Alberta spread her fingers in denial. "I'll be the cat among the pigeons. No one will be able to say for sure what role I played."

Maggie pointed her pencil at each one in turn. "Do we all understand this? We're not to say a word to anyone, not our neighbours, not our husbands, and especially none of the pastorate or Aggie Waters."

"We'll all be standing in the need of prayer if this falls apart," said Alberta. "Me especially."

"Is everyone agreed?" Maggie patted Alberta's arm and looked around the table. Heads nodded in agreement. "Good! We'll let the others know in due time, so they won't be able to spill the beans for lack of time. In the meantime we'll go about our work as we always have. I think we've done all we can this evening. I'll call this meeting to a close."

"We'll never speak of this inside the church," said Lizzie. "If we have news we'll meet here."

Alberta finished typing the sixth version of the pageant. She stretched her arms over her head to ease the ache. I hope this strike thing works, she thought. She stretched her back muscles, first left, then right.

The office door opened letting in the late autumn air. Alberta looked up. "Maggie! I didn't think I'd be seeing you today. What's up?" She clutched her papers that lifted in the draft.

"Nothing much. I came for the auditions. I want to play Mary." She settled herself on an office chair and unbuttoned her coat.

"Really?" Alberta looked her friend up and down.

"Yes," said Maggie, "I've always wanted that role ever since we started doing pageant."

"Don't you think you're a little old for that?"

Maggie shrugged. "Makeup can do wonders. Besides, I think we need another cat."

"In that case, you'll be a wonderful Mary." Alberta tidied the papers on her desk. "Hang your coat up and come talk to me while I make fifteen more copies." She shook her head. "I hope that's the last time I have to do this."

"How many times is this?" Maggie shrugged out of her coat and hung it on the rack behind the door.

Alberta sighed. "The sixth, I think. I wasn't counting." She stood and led the way to the copier closet. "I sure hope this works."

"Do you really have to do fifteen copies?" Maggie held the door to the tiny room that housed the copy machine for Alberta.

Alberta nodded. "It's two more than I had to have last week." She laid the originals face down on the top tray and punched a few buttons. Presently the machine began to print.

Maggie picked up the first page as it came warm from the printer. She began to read. Her eyebrows rose high above her glasses. "He fancies himself a writer, doesn't he?"

Alberta nodded. "I think fancy is the right word for it."

"Or maybe fantasy." Maggie continued reading. "My goodness, where does he think he'll get camels from at this short notice?"

"He just waved his magic finger in my direction and poof, I made them appear." Alberta collected the finished pages from the tray and began checking them for accuracy. "Actually I didn't. I know a man who breeds them for zoos, and he has three that are tame—well, as tame as camels can get." She thumped the pages into neatness. "However, I didn't tell Jarrod yet that I had them."

"Making him sweat, are you?" Maggie raised one eyebrow.

"Just a little. He deserves it, don't you think?" Alberta took another stack of pages from the copier and thumped them onto the others in the stack. "I'll get some of the kids to help me collate these."

"It's too bad the church can't spring for a new machine that collates this stuff for you." Maggie took up another page and glanced down the script. "It's the least they could do, and it would make your job a lot easier."

Alberta sniffed. "Pastor Teddy tried to but Momma Aggie said it was a waste of money and that I could do it in my spare time."

"Wouldn't you know she'd have something to say about it." Maggie frowned at the absent Aggie.

"That's the way it's always been," said Alberta.

"Aggie's always had hold of the purse strings and she's as tight as drum. You can't get a nickle out of her when she takes a notion to it. D'you remember old Mr. Smithson?"

"Sort of. He was the original caretaker here wasn't he?"

Alberta nodded. "He's dead now, of course, but he needed to replace the vacuum cleaner, and the lawn was getting to be too much for him just using the push mower."

"Didn't he take over from Teddy after he retired from his job at the department store?"

"That's him." Alberta lifted another handful of papers from the copier and laid them on top of the stack. "He put in a request to buy a new vacuum and another to buy a gas mower and Aggie got wind of it and threw a fit. So once again Teddy knuckled under to dear old Mummy."

"And Mr. Smithson?"

"Poor Mr. Smithson worked for another year, and

one of the elders found him in back of the church slumped over the mower."

"What was he doing?"

"He'd been mowing, and it was very hot and humid. He shouldn't have been doing it at all, and except for Aggie, he wouldn't have."

"They weren't able to save him?" The copier ceased its copying and spit out the last page. Alberta picked them up and added them to her pile. She shook her head. "No, they weren't. He was already gone. The autopsy said it was a heart attack brought on by heavy exertion in the heat and humidity." Alberta sniffed softly. "And butter wouldn't have melted in Aggie's mouth. She sat up front with the mourners and wielded her handkerchief like a pro. After all, she'd known him since she was a child."

"Who performed the ceremony?"

"In his will he had asked for Mr. Thomas, the lay preacher, to do the honours. They were great friends, you know. Aggie was spitting mad. She thought Teddy should have done it, but Teddy couldn't have anyway because he was home nursing a migraine." Alberta slammed the door to the copy room and stalked up the hall.

"He seems to be afflicted with them frequently," said Maggie.

"Indeed, he does." Alberta opened the door to her office and ushered Maggie in. "I guess I'd better collate these myself. It'll likely be too late when the kids get here."

Chapter 3

"Your will be done," intoned Jarrod, "Amen."

"Amen," chorused the assembly. Jarrod raised his head and looked over the crowd. "So everyone wants a part in the play. Well, there are only ten roles to share and how many hopefuls do we have here?" He began counting heads. "I can see there will be many disappointments, so brace yourselves for the inevitable. Those who want to play Joseph, come with me." He strode to the door of the classroom. "Those of you who want to play Mary, practise your parts. I'll audition you next."

The group bent their heads to the task of memorizing the dialogue. Presently the door opened and Jarrod stuck his head into the room. "Marys, come with me."

Maggie and a half dozen others rose and followed Jarrod to the auditorium.

"It's a little early to be measuring for costumes, Miss Maggie," said Jarrod.

Maggie cleared her throat. "I'm here to audition for the part."

Jarrod snickered behind his sheaf of pages. "Aren't you a little old to be Mary? You must be approaching seventy at least."

Maggie's chin rose an inch and she looked at Jarrod.

"Sixty, and you said yourself that stage makeup can do the impossible." She stepped past him with her head held so high she stepped on his toes.

"Ouch!" Jarrod hopped on one foot and shook the injured one.

"Excuse me, Jarrod, I didn't mean to hurt you." Her brown eyes gleamed with mischief.

He raised his head and looked at her. "You did so," he said. "Just for that you can audition last." He closed the door behind the stragglers. He limped up the aisle clapping his hands for order. "Quiet everyone! This is a very important role and I will choose whomever I think is best." His glance took in Maggie. Pure spite gleamed in his pale blue eyes. "I'll take you as I call you." He scanned down the list and called two names.

"I'll read the other parts and you respond as Mary. I'll hear you first, Allison."

A thin pale twelve year old took the stage and made reply to Jarrod's Joseph in almost a monotone.

"Thank you," said Jarrod. "That's all I need to hear." He ticked her name off the list then called, "Barbie! You're next."

He proceeded through the list with speed. At the end he said: "Thank you, everyone. The list will be available on the bulletin board tomorrow. Only those listed need be present at the rehearsal."

He turned to go. Maggie rose and stood in his path. "I believe I have a right to be auditioned too," she said.

"You can audition as much as you want but make it fast. I have several more characters to hear." He pushed past her and opened the door. "In any case, I have already decided who gets the part." He allowed the door to swing shut on his giggle.

"I don't need your silly old part anyway," muttered

Maggie. "That wasn't the reason I was here at all, so you can just wait and take your medicine with the rest of the leadership."

Molly and Lucy sat on the edge of the stage where they had been for both auditions. "He's despicable," said Lucy. "Whatever made him think he'd make a good minister?"

Molly chuckled. "No one we know. I wonder what Larry would say about him."

"He's an ignoramus. Has been since he was born. He was a breech birth, you know." Larry's voice boomed out of the shadows created by the stage curtains.

Molly and Lucy startled."I wish you wouldn't do that," said Molly.

"Just keeping you on your collective toes," replied Larry.

He held onto his Gainsborough hat with the red plume in it and jumped to the floor.

"How'd you know we were here?" asked Lucy.

"I was in the neighbourhood and I figured out where you would be. Besides, you did file your flight plan, for once."

"Well, excuse me," said Molly. "I was only doing as I had been told." She hitched herself into a more comfortable position on the edge of the stage. "Did you want me for something?"

"I was going to ask you to come with me to the Spirit Ball next week," said Larry. "I thought you might like to get out for a few hours."

For once Molly was practically speechless. "I—Lucy—you?"

"Yes, you," said Larry. "Lucy won't mind anyway." He turned toward Lucy. "You won't will you, Lucy?"

"Of course not," said Lucy. "Molly hasn't been anywhere in ages. It's about time she got out."

"So, Molly, can I take that as a yes?" asked Larry.

Molly's mouth was still agape. She shut it with a click and then swallowed. "I—I guess so."

Larry swept his voluminous cape around his shoulders and swept off his hat. "I do thank you in advance, Madam." He bowed to Molly. "I am looking forward to a week from Friday. Good evening to you both." He floated up to the stage and disappeared on his way to the shadow of the curtains.

Molly blinked as she watched the red egret feather in Larry's cap dissolve into mist and then disappear. "What's come over him?"

"I told you so," said Lucy. Her smile was wide. "I told you that when you first started coming to this side of the veil."

"You did?" Molly looked at her friend.

"I did. D'you remember I told you about Christena making a play for him?"

"Vaguely," said Molly.

"Well, she made such a pest of herself that Larry went to the elders and complained. They took it seriously because it was Larry who was complaining and sent her on a long assignment mentoring a baby who was born blind. She's always been good with children."

"Humph," said Molly. "I bet she liked that."

"She adjusted. She's learned not to chase powerful men."

"Especially Larry," said Molly. "Why didn't I hear of this before?"

"It happened when you were vacationing on Jupiter." The door to the auditorium opened and another troupe of potential actors came in with Jarrod in the lead.

"Find yourself a place to sit. I'll hear your scenes in the order in which they appear."

"I guess that's our cue to split," said Molly. "He carries bad vibes no matter what he's doing."

Lucy made a face. "Nor how hard he tries." Together Molly and Lucy floated past Jarrod and through the back wall.

Jarrod shivered and called the first name.

"Well, hello there, Barbara Ann. How are you?" asked Alberta. She stuck the pencils she had been sharpening into the mug that said Grand Canyon across a map of Arizona.

Barbara dried her shoes on the welcome mat. "I'm fine, Miss Alberta." A slight frown creased her freckled forehead.

"What brings you here today?" Alberta picked up the letters for the bulk mailing that was to go out in the morning. She banged them on the desk to tidy the stack.

"I just got off work at the shelter." Barbara Ann rubbed her nose with the back of her hand then inspected the trail of mucus that covered the back to her wrist. She sniffed hard.

Alberta shuddered slightly and handed Barbara Ann the box of tissues. "You got away a little earlier than you usually do."

"I wasn't supposed to leave," she said. "The others were making fun of me." She rubbed her hands together to restore a little warmth to them. She began folding letters and stuffing envelopes. "They were making fun of the way I talk. And the way I walk." Barbara Ann picked a letter off Alberta's pile and began folding it into thirds. "I don't think I walk funny. D'you, Miss Alberta?"

"Of course, not, nor talk funny either. Sometimes we have to wait for you to pull your thoughts together, but it's always worth the wait." Alberta patted Barbara Ann's arm well above the snot line. "Don't you listen to them. They're not as hot as they think they are, and you can tell them I said so."

"Oh, Miss Alberta, I wouldn't tell them that." She put the letter she had folded onto the stack that Alberta was building.

"You did a fine job of folding that letter," said Alberta. "Can I recruit you as a volunteer for the rest of the afternoon?"

Barbara Ann squinted her eyes and looked at Alberta. "What's 'recute' mean?"

"It means to offer someone a job. It's pronounced recruit." Alberta picked up a stack of letters and a box of envelopes and carried them to a small work table in the corner of the office. "You do a fine job of folding and stuffing. How'd you get that good?"

Barbara Ann's smile was wide and her ruddy cheeks turned a brighter shade of rose. "We do this kind of work at the shelter all the time. That's how we earn our allowance."

Alberta pulled up a metal chair for each of them. "If you don't mind helping, we'll have this job done in jig time."

"What's jig time?" Barbara Ann pulled her chair close to the table.

"It means to get something done in a short time." Alberta divided the stack between them and they began folding and stuffing.

Presently Barbara Ann said: "I think I'd like to be baptized."

"Oh?" Alberta's hands were still for a moment.

"Yes. " Barbara Ann nodded her head. "I want to be baptized."

"You know what that means, do you?"

"It means that I'll be a child of God and I won't have to be ashamed no more." Barbara Ann's hands kept busy at their task. "They won't be able to make fun of me at the shelter, and Pastor Jarrod won't be able to talk behind my back and call me names because I'll be God's child."

"What's Pastor Jarrod been saying?" Alberta began folding letters again.

Barbara Ann shrugged and sighed. "He calls me Big Red all the time, and he sets me up to be an idiot and everyone laughs, but I don't see the joke until I've had time to think about it, and sometimes it's the next day before I get it." She sighed again. "Then I feel real bad, like I really am just a moron."

Alberta reached over and put her arms around Barbara Ann. "First of all, you're not a moron. You just need a little help to get by. Second of all, your hair is beautiful. It's lovely and thick and a wonderful shade of copper than exactly matches your freckles. I'll have a word with Pastor Jarrod about this."

Barbara Ann pulled out of Alberta's embrace. "D'you think that'll work? Then maybe you can come down to the shelter and tell the others that I'm not funny looking, because I'm not."

Alberta pursed her lips. "I don't know how much influence I'll have at the shelter. They don't know me from Adam. But I'll certainly have a word with Pastor Jarrod."

"Have a word with Pastor Jarrod about what?"

Alberta startled. "I didn't hear you come in."

"Obviously not." Jarrod dropped the stack of church newsletters on top of Alberta's work. "But that's no surprise as I was already in. I was giving Pastor Sam the music I want for the pageant. I hope he does a better job with it this year than last." He turned to leave. "Those newsletters can go out with whatever you're mailing. It'll save my department some money."

Alberta watched Jarrod out of sight down the hall.

"What department?" asked Barbara Ann.

"Sh-h!" Alberta put her finger to her lips until she was sure Jarrod was out of earshot. She lowered her voice. "I wonder what size his britches are?"

Barbara Ann giggled. "Too small."

"He doesn't have a department. He just thinks he does. A department is more than just one person."

"Am I too fat, Miss Alberta?" She frowned. "Maybe I deserve to be called Big Red."

"Barbara Ann! You are no such thing. You're pleasingly plump and that's all. Don't ever let me hear you put yourself down again. Especially for people like Jarrod." Alberta pulled her pencil from behind her ear and picked up a notebook. I'll speak to Pastor Waters about your baptism."

"Pastor Waters? I'd like a word with you if you have a moment." Alberta opened the office door and caught Teddy lacing his coffee from a silver flask.

"Pastor Waters! What are you doing?"

"Just a medithinal drop to keep away the cold." Teddy glanced up at Alberta from watery blue eyes. He blinked and looked away. "Are you going to tell the powers that be?"

Alberta shook her head. "Why would I do that? You're never under the influence in the pulpit, and you preach a fine sermon."

Teddy's ruddy face turned a little more ruddy. "Do I? It'th hard to tell thometimes." He licked his dry lips and hiccuped. "I mothtly just read. I can't seem to find the right words thomehow. Even when Mummy coacheth me." He sipped at his steaming cup.

Alberta pulled up a chair and sat down across the desk from Teddy. "I've brought a request for a baptism."

Teddy set his cup down and sat up straighter. "You do? How wonderful! Hardly anyone wanths to be baptithed these dayth." His colorless eyes seemed to hold a sparkle. "Who ith it?"

"Barbara Ann Milliman."

"Oh." Teddy's body sagged back into his chair. He picked up his mug and took another sip. "I gueth that's better than no one." He sighed. "I don't theem to be able to convict anyone these dayth.

Alberta raised one bushy gray eyebrow. "I don't

suppose it ever occurred to you that less of the tonic and a little more effort on your part might reverse that trend?"

Teddy dropped his chin onto his chest. "I jutht want to make Mummy proud of me."

"Mission impossible." Alberta shook her head. "If you haven't made your mother proud by now it's never going to happen." She laid the sheaf of papers pertaining to Barbara Ann's baptism on the desk. "Barbara Ann will be ready on Sunday."

Alberta walked down the hallway to Pastor Jarrod's office and rapped on the door.

"Come in." Jarrod's voice sounded muffled.

Alberta entered and glanced around the room. "Pastor Jarrod? Are you here?"

Jarrod stuck his head up from behind the desk. "I'm here."

"Getting in a little prayer time, are you?" Alberta's lips twitched in her effort not to smile.

Jarrod scowled. "Of course, not. I dropped the box of sequins that go on the edge of the magis' capes." He disappeared beneath the desk again. "You might at least help me. There must be two thousand of them."

Alberta leaned over the front of his desk. "You need a broom and dustpan." She brushed a stack of play manuscripts and they began a slow cascade to the floor. "Oops, I didn't mean to do that." Mischief sparkled in her eyes.

Jarrod's sigh of long suffering gusted from beneath the desk. "I said help, not hinder, Miss Alberta."

"I'll get the broom and dustpan." Alberta hurried out of the office before she could make any more mess. Presently she returned with the broom. "I couldn't find the dustpan," she said.

"That's likely because the janitor has it." Jarrod's pale features grew redder in his frustration. "Here's a piece of paper. It's thick enough to work for a dustpan." He crawled out from under his desk and stood up, his face paling as he did so. "I'll be back in a few minutes,

Miss Alberta." He strode out of the office. "Don't throw those out. We are on a limited budget."

Alberta rolled her eyes. "As if I would without asking," she muttered. "And why do I get the job cleaning up after Pastor Jarrod?" She knelt behind the desk and began sweeping at the multi-colored sequins.

Jarrod returned just as Alberta finished the sweeping. "Oh, good. You've gotten them all up. You're a marvel, Miss Alberta.

Alberta looked at him and frowned. "Thank you, Jarrod. That's the nicest thing you've ever said to me." She dumped the sequins into a manila envelope. "Now, I must have a word with you." She sat down in his office chair. "It has come to my attention that you've been calling people names."

Jarrod stepped behind his desk and towered over Alberta so that she had to tip her head back. "Who told you that?"

"Never mind the source, I just heard it." She rolled the chair backward to get out from under Jarrod's threatening stance.

"No one that I know then." Jarrod stepped forward again.

Alberta stood up and looked Jarrod in the eye. "It doesn't matter who told me. I have never found the person to be untruthful."

Jarrod stood looking at Alberta for a full minute before saying anything.

I can hear the wheels turning, thought Alberta.

"If you can't tell me who told you, who was I supposed to have called names?"

"Barbara Ann. My informant said that you call her 'Big Red' and set her up to be the butt of jokes that she doesn't understand."

"That moron ... "

Alberta seemed to grow taller as her indignation increased. "She is not a moron. She's a wonderful, kindhearted young woman, and you have no right to treat her that way. If I ever hear another report about name-calling, Barbara Ann or anyone else, I will take it up with the board of elders."

Jarrod snorted. "Much good that'll do you. They haven't done anything decisive in the five years I've been here. I don't know how this church accomplishes anything." Jarrod held the door open. "Good night, Miss Alberta. Have a good one."

"Have a good one," repeated Alberta when she'd gotten out of earshot of Jarrod. She accompanied the sentiment with a nasty face that was intercepted by Sam as she rounded the corner to her office.

"Oops," said Sam. "I'm glad I'm not the recipient of that face."

"Oh, Pastor Sam, good day." She shook her head. "Pastor Jarrod has reached the end of my patience." Alberta relaxed her face into a smile. "He needs to be called up short on his behaviour."

Sam raised both eyebrows. "Oh?"

She nodded. "He's so rude and to people who don't deserve it."

Sam held the door to the office open and stood aside to allow Alberta to enter before him. "Like who?"

"Barbara Ann. He's been calling her names and setting her up for ridicule in front of everyone."

"But Barbara Ann is so kind and gentle, why would he want to do that?" Sam pulled the door shut behind himself.

"I guess, because she's simple, and he can."

"But that's just bullying."

Alberta shrugged. "That's what I mean. She was asking about baptism this afternoon. She thinks that it will cause Jarrod and a few others at the shelter to have a little more respect for her. I didn't disabuse her of the idea."

"No point," replied Sam. "She'll find out sooner or later." He hitched one of the chairs in front of the desk and sat down. "Who's going to do it?"

"Pastor Waters, if he's available. Otherwise I don't know who. It may have to be postponed." Alberta sat down behind her desk and leaned her elbows on the edge of it. "His vitamins may get the best of him at the last minute."

Sam suppressed a snort of derision. "I guess I shouldn't be surprised. It is the fall, and the cold and flu season is upon us. I wonder what he takes in the spring."

Alberta's eyes gleamed. "Probably sulfur and molasses in juice."

"Does Mummy know?"

"If she does, she's not saying."

"Why does he still have a pulpit?"

"Because no one has the heart to take it to the board of trustees." Alberta dropped her chin into her cupped hand. "Besides, Jarrod wants the pulpit next and we don't want him."

"I see." Sam picked up a pencil from the Arizona mug and began doodling on the edge of Alberta's desk pad. "Well, there's not much to be done in that case." His drawing began to take the shape of a flop-eared mule with Jarrod's features.

Alberta took the pencil from him and put it back in

the mug. "So what brings you to my office?"

Sam's face flushed a little. "How well do you know Jane?"

"D'you mean Jane Ridgeway?"

Sam nodded. "Well enough, I suppose. We've been friends ever since she came to teach at the college. She came to be with me when my mother died. That's ten years ago now."

"What's she like?" Sam tucked his hands between his knees to still the fine tremor that seemed to have taken them over.

"She's a good solid friend. Straightforward, too. She dated one of the science professors up at the college for a short time, but that kind of fizzled out."

"So she's not seeing anyone now?"

"I don't think so. Pastor Jarrod asked her out a couple of times but she'd never go with him. She's very astute when it comes to people. She saw Jarrod for what he is the first time she laid eyes on him."

"She's smart then."

"Oh, yes. She can't abide phonies, nor people who practise deceit."

Chapter 4

"You know," said Lucy, "we could influence Pastor Jarrod to change." She sat on top of the war memorial and swung her feet in circles.

"I thought we weren't supposed to interfere," said Molly. She floated from her perch on the other end of war memorial and settled on the branch of the willow tree dark with the closing year.

Lucy shrugged. "I wasn't thinking of that exactly. I just meant that we could, perhaps, alter his opinion of himself a little. But maybe not."

"I think with Larry dropping in any time he feels like it, that we'd better leave that one alone. Remember what happened the last time."

Lucy laughed. "I know. I didn't think they'd keep you in solitary for such a long time."

"Well, they did, and it was no laughing matter." Molly scowled at the memory.

"Anyway, I was thinking of us doing a little persuasion, like we did to Gertrude."

Molly pursed her lips. "That might be feasible. We can haunt him day and night." She nodded. "Yes, that would work."

"Pastor Waters could use a little persuading too," said Lucy. She floated down from the war memorial and landed gently on the brown grass.

"I don't think so." Molly shook her head. "He's a sick man and it might not take too much to push him over the edge."

"Not even a pastoral visitation?" Lucy's blue eyes sparkled.

Molly grimaced at this idea. "Maybe. But just a brief one."

"Oh, goody! Let's drop in on him now."

Molly slid down from the willow branch she was sitting on. "He'll just be having his morning coffee."

Molly and Lucy arranged themselves side by side on the love seat in Pastor Waters' office.

"One for the money, two for the show," Teddy sang softly to himself as he poured his 'vitamins' into his coffee. "Three to get ready, and four to go." He stirred in two lumps of sugar. "And here's to you, Mummy. How I wish you were sometimes."

"Wish she were what?" asked Lucy from her end of the love seat.

"A mummy," said Molly.

"But I thought he was fond of his mother," said Lucy.

"So did I," said Molly, "but I guess we were wrong." She settled her red and yellow caftan more comfortably around her knees. She shook the matching scarf that she was wearing on her head over her shoulder, then crossed her legs at the ankle and turned her attention toward Teddy once more.

Presently the office door swung open and Aggie hobbled in pushing her walker in front of herself. "Here, Teddy, you forgot these." She handed Pastor Waters a sheaf of papers.

"You need to be practising this before Sunday."

Pastor Waters shuffled through the pages. "That was last week's sermon."

Aggie settled herself on the love seat between Molly and Lucy. "I declare, this sofa is getting more and more uncomfortable every time I sit on it."

"Hey, watch where you're sitting, lady," said Molly.

"And who you're sitting on," added Lucy. She wriggled out from under the edge of Aggie's bulk and smoothed her poodle skirt then straightened her blue twin set around her waist.

"Did you say something, Teddy dear?"

"No, Mummy, I was justh reading the introduction over again, I may have thaid a word or two aloud." He turned a page and continued reading. "Help yourself to the coffee. It's fresh."

"Thanks, I will have a cup, if you'd be so kind," said Aggie.

Pastor Waters continued to read.

"Teddy!"

Pastor Waters startled and knocked over his coffee

cup. "Yeth, Mother." He began dabbing at the mess with a handful of tissues.

"Are you going to pour me a cup of coffee or not?"

"Yeth, Mother, in a moment." Pastor Waters' cleanup effort was not going well.

"I said now, Teddy. I don't have all day to waste."

Pastor Waters jumped again. "Certainly, Mother. How would you like it today?" He pulled a new cup from the stack and filled it with steaming coffee. "What'th your hurry today?"

"I haven't finished proofing next Sunday's sermon for you."

Teddy's shoulders slumped. "I with you wouldn't do that, Mummy. Mith Alberta ith quite capable of proof-reading for me. That'th what we pay her for."

Molly and Lucy looked at one another. "So that's how she does it," said Molly.

"Clever!" said Lucy. "Getting her version of the sermon in on Sundays."

"She's a frustrated preacher," said Molly.

"We'll have to do something about that," said Lucy.

"She'd probably benefit from a little visit herself," said Molly. She rubbed her hands together in anticipation. "C'mon, Lucy, this vacation won't be so dull after all."

"Who should we take on first?" asked Molly.

"That depends," said Larry. "Who is it going to have the most effect on, and who needs it the most?" He eased his bulk onto one of the tombstones and settled his second best cloak around himself. "These tombstones are getting harder every year."

Molly sat on the stone opposite Larry, and Lucy sat beside her. "I hadn't thought about that before," she said. "I'd vote for Teddy. He's the one who most needs bracing up."

"Pastor Jarrod just needs a complete makeover, and Aggie needs a good scare." Molly turned toward Lucy. "What do you think?"

"You're going to have to be a little gentle with Pastor

Waters. He's not too far from going over the edge now." Lucy's brow wrinkled with worry for Teddy.

"He's stronger than he thinks he is," said Molly. "We just need to convince him of that."

Lucy's forehead wrinkled even more. "I know, but supposing we're wrong and he really does lose it. We'll be responsible for it and him too."

"What'll happen to us in case something awful happens?"

The evening breeze picked up the tail of Molly's scarf and streamed it out behind her. "Y'know our motto is to help and not hurt." She grabbed at her scarf and wound it more warmly around her neck and stuffed the ends inside her coat.

"D'you remember the time you spent in solitary confinement?" Larry smirked at Molly.

"Humph!" said Molly. "I don't need you to remind me."

"It'll be much longer before you see sunlight again. It will also be a lot darker while you're there. So you two had better come up with a plan that won't be a disaster in the making." Larry stood up and swirled his navy cape around his shoulders. "I must be off. Don't do anything without letting me know first." He turned and floated down the central path toward the cemetery gate, the rustle of the dead leaves the only sign of his passing.

Molly stuck her tongue out at Larry's departing figure. As the red plume of his Gainsborough hat melted into the sunset, Molly made a face and mocked Larry, "Don't do anything without letting me know first."

Lucy giggled. "C'mon, Molly, don't be rude. You know he wants the best for us, and he did invite you to the Spirit Ball."

Molly groaned. "And I said I'd go, didn't I?"

"You'll have a good time, and Larry's good fun when he wants to be."

Molly slid down off her perch and brushed at the lichens stuck to her coat. "We'd better get down to brass tacks and start planning the haunting."

"I'd like to start this evening," said Lucy. "Tonight's

prayer meeting and they'll all be there." She bent to straighten her nylons. "It's the perfect opportunity."

Molly nodded. "You're right. We shouldn't let any opportunity slip by. Let's go and see what Pastor Teddy's doing."

Teddy pulled into the parking slot marked 'Pastor' and turned off the engine of his ancient car. "I don't know why they don't allot me a car allowance," he muttered. He picked up the foam cup holding half a quart of coffee from the convenience store near his home. He hefted it in one hand to determine how much coffee was left. "Just enough," he said softly to himself. He opened the car door and struggled out of the driver's seat at the same time being careful not to spill his coffee. "A few vitaminth won't come amith on this cold evening."

Molly and Lucy followed his bulky form into the church. Teddy fumbled with the keys to his office, and Molly and Lucy sifted through the wall and settled themselves side by side on the love seat.

"Vitaminth vitaminth, lovely vitaminth." Teddy finally got the key to work for him and he hastened into his office shedding his coat as he came. He tossed it onto the love seat.

"Hey, fella," said Molly. She wriggled out from under the pastor's winter coat, "you don't need to smother us." She pulled the coat away from Lucy. "Are you okay?"

"Yes, thank you." Lucy straightened her sweater more neatly around her hips, then ran her fingers through her hair.

"It's too warm in here to wear a coat," said Molly. "I'll just dump it on the floor."

Pastor Teddy turned just in time to see his coat slide to the floor in an untidy heap. "Drat," he said with little conviction. He picked up the coat and flung it back onto Molly's lap.

"I said cut it out." Molly raised her voice and threw the coat on the floor again.

Teddy watched the coat cascading to the floor. He blinked and looked again. He picked up the coat and put it on the love seat once more.

Molly concentrated her energy and pushed the coat off again. "I said, cut it out. Are you deaf or something?"

Teddy circled the coat. He studied it from several angles then picked it up by the left sleeve. He tossed it onto the sofa again.

"Don't," shouted Lucy and pushed the coat off one more time.

Teddy rubbed his ears and looked into all the corners of the office.

"I'm not there," said Molly. "I'm right here." She picked up the coat and hung it on the coat rack.

Teddy gasped and swallowed hard. He shook his head.

"Maybe I've had too many vitaminth lately." His voice shook.

"Or maybe not enough," said Molly. She sat down by Lucy on the sofa. "I wish I could make him hear better."

Lucy giggled. "You could use some of those vitamins yourself."

"Can I draw a little energy from you? I haven't needed

this much energy since we were convincing Gertrude."

"By all means," said Lucy. She picked up Molly's hand and concentrated on sending her energy.

Teddy turned to his desk and sat in the black leather desk chair. His eyes never left his coat. "I must have hung it there mythelf and just forgot I'd done it," he said.

"No such luck, Teddy dear." Molly's voice came from the direction of the sofa. "I hung it up for you."

Pastor Waters rubbed at his right ear, then dug a plug of wax from the depths of his ear canal. He rubbed it onto the lining of his coat. He cocked his head to listen. The room was silent. He rubbed his ears again. "I must be hearing thingth. He opened his eyes wide and stared in the direction of the love seat. The shadows seemed to move and float, then settle. He opened the desk drawer and lifted out his bottle of vitamins, then poured a generous dose into his convenience store coffee. He stopped pouring and set the bottle on the desk and stared once more into the shadows of the love seat. The vague outline of a woman's face seemed to take shape and then dissipate. He picked up the vitamins and filled the cup to the brim and downed several gulps of it at once. He coughed, then sat up straight in his chair. "I'm imagining thingth," he said.

"No, you're not," said Molly. "You're still of sound mind, at least. We won't mention what shape your body's in."

"Huh." Teddy's eyes bulged. He rose from his chair and sidled past the love seat to turn on the overhead light.

"That won't do you a bit of good, you know," said Molly. Her voice came and went. "Drat, I'm losing power," she said to Lucy.

"So'm I," said Lucy. She let go of Molly's hand. "That's all I can give you for now." Her face was pale and strained.

Molly looked at her. "Why didn't you stop me? I could have saved this for another day."

"The situation was too perfect to pass up." Colour

was returning to Lucy's face. "I'm tired. I need some sustenance before we tackle Aggie and Jarrod."

"I always carry a snack when I travel. You never know how long it will be until lunch." Molly rummaged in the folds of her yellow caftan. "You never know what they'll serve you either." She pulled out an unopened package of trail mix.

"Here, try this. It'll get you home at least."

Lucy's hands shook as she struggled with the heat seal of the package.

"Here, let me." Molly opened the package with a quick turn of her fingers on the seal. "That really drained you."

Lucy nodded. "I don't very often have to share energy with someone." She bit into a slice of dried banana.

"You don't have a whole lot of energy to spare anyway. We won't do that again."

"Except in an emergency." She leaned back against the sofa. "I'll just rest a moment before we take on Pastor Jarrod."

"I'll need some prayer if this Christmas pageant is going to come off." Jarrod rummaged through the papers on his desk sending half the stack cascading to the floor. "Hell and damnation," he muttered, then glanced at the door to his office still ajar from his entrance. "Miss Alberta, where are you when I need you?" He continued his haphazard search of his desk.

"Need some help, Pastor Jarrod?" Molly leaned against the desk and gave a gentle push to the remaining folders. They joined the others on the floor. "You know this is not the place to use unpleasant language." Molly perched on the edge of the desk and watched Jarrod.

"I'll say what I want," said Jarrod, then looked around to see who he was talking to. There was no one visible. He shrugged his shoulders and returned to his task.

"Is this what you're looking for?" said Molly.

Jarrod watched a piece of paper rise from the floor, pause for a moment then flutter down onto the desk. He stared at the paper with the telephone numbers he was looking for. He picked it up by the edge and looked at both sides of it.

"It's really yours," said Molly. She blew down Jarrod's neck. He shivered then bent to pick up the folders and threw them any which way onto the desk. He pocketed the list and went out closing the door behind himself.

"Time for prayer meeting," said Molly. "I wonder if Aggie will mind if I sit next to her."

"As long as you don't squirm," said Lucy. She floated beside Molly into the sanctuary. "I don't see her."

"She's over there talking to Lizzie." Molly gestured toward the next aisle.

"Lizzie doesn't appear to be liking the conversation."

"Would you?" asked Molly. "It's an experience I'll pass on for now."

Aggie sidled into the pew and Lizzie moved down a space or two to make room for Aggie. Molly and Lucy settled themselves on either side of Aggie. Aggie talked on, oblivious to the extra company in the pew.

"I sure miss Libby since she passed on," said Aggie.

Lizzie turned her hearing aid up and turned her ear

toward Aggie. "Excuse me, Aggie, I didn't hear what you said."

"You don't half listen," said Aggie. "I don't know why you bother with that thing, it never works right."

"It works fine if I'm not being shouted at," said Lizzy. She turned the hearing aid down again.

"Good for you, Lizzy," said Molly. "You put her in her place if she still knows where her place is."

Lucy clapped silently in approval.

"Is that a clap offering you're giving?" asked Molly. She joined in the applause.

"Oh, yes. She deserves one for standing up to Aggie."

"I said, I sure miss Libby since she passed on." Aggie raised her voice another decibel.

"I'm sorry, Aggie, I still can't hear you." Lizzy turned away from Aggie to talk to her right hand neighbour. "How are you, Sandra? I meant to greet you on Sunday but by the time I got to where I'd seen you, you were gone."

"She can hear well when she wants to," said Aggie

to no one in particular. She hitched herself around and stared straight ahead.

"Y'know, Libby should be here to talk to Aggie. They were best friends so Aggie says."

"That's not what Libby says," said Molly. "In any case, I'm not sure she has enough power to bridge the gap."

"Can you mimic her?" In her excitement, Lucy started to bounce in her seat.

Aggie looked from right to left but saw no reason why her seat should be bouncing. "Kids," she muttered.

Molly pursed her lips and thought for a moment. "I can mimic the sound of her voice, but I doubt I could mimic her presentation."

"What if Libby told you what to say? Could you do it then?"

"That's a good idea that's only getting better." Molly's eyes sparkled. "Next Sunday we'll all come to church."

"In the meantime we could prepare the ground, so to speak." Lucy rubbed her hands together in anticipation.

"You're becoming quite the little instigator," said

Larry. "Who'd have thought that our sweet gentle Lucy would be thinking up these kinds of schemes."

"Not I." Molly rolled her eyes.

Lucy ducked her head. "I discovered how much fun it was, working with Gertrude. And ultimately we do a lot of good." She peeked up at Larry and Molly.

"That's true, said Molly. "But sometimes it's by the skin of our teeth, so we don't want to crow too loudly."

"Lets hear your plan," said Larry. He settled his bulk on the next pew. Around them prayer meeting continued as always.

"I thought we might make ourselves known to a number of people who need to be brought up short." Molly fanned through a hymnal looking for the hymn.

"Who in particular?" asked Larry.

"Jarrod, Aggie and Pastor Teddy."

"He promised never to leave me, never to leave me alone," sang the congregation.

"Aggie's always out of tune." Lucy shook her head.

"I suppose we could teach her to sing," said Molly.

Larry drew his eyebrows into a straight line and shook his finger at them. "Listen you two. Don't you do anything that I have to bail you out of. The last time I pulled your irons from the fire I nearly had to pay for it myself. And you, Molly, know from experience what it's like to spend time in solitary. So behave yourselves."

"Yes, Larry," said Lucy, "We'll be good."

"Speak for yourself," said Molly. "I intend to give them a haunting they'll not soon forget."

"Molly!" Lucy's cry was fearful.

"Oh, don't worry." Molly waved her right hand in dismissal. "I won't do anything too bad. I won't inflict any bodily harm."

"No harm at all," said Larry.

"Yield not to temptation," sang the congregation.

"Of course not," said Molly. "We'll just give them something to think about." Aggie moved her rump and sat squarely on Molly's lap.

"Ow!" said Molly. "Get off me you great elephant." She pushed hard on Aggie's bum. Aggie squirmed to gain a more comfortable seat. Molly pinched Aggie hard on the flesh that was pinning her to the pew.

"Ow!" said Aggie. She stood and knocked her purse to the floor. She turned to look at her space on the pew.

"You have a request?" asked Sam.

"No!" said Aggie.

"A testimony, perhaps." Jarrod came toward her with the microphone.

Aggie pushed the microphone aside and reached for her purse.

Molly handed the purse to Aggie.

Aggie startled, then looked at the empty space beside her on the pew.

"Perhaps it's this you're looking for." Molly passed Aggie the compact and lipstick that had rolled onto the floor.

Aggie stood staring at her lipstick hovering in thin air.

Jarrod pushed the microphone toward her once more. "Are you sure you don't have a testimony,

Sister Aggie?"

Aggie grabbed for her lipstick and compact. "Certainly not!" She sat down in her seat and stuffed the cosmetics back into her purse.

"If you're sure." Jarrod waved the microphone in the air. Sam played the opening measures of "Rescue the Perishing." The congregation took up the song from long habit.

"Jarrod, just go away," said Aggie. "You're an ass."

"Way to go," said Molly in Aggie's left ear.

Aggie rubbed her ear and looked down at the empty pew. She rubbed her ear again.

"Go Aggie," said Molly.

Aggie gave another look at the empty pew, unfolded her walker, hung her purse across her bosom and stalked out of the sanctuary. Pastor Teddy followed closely on her heels.

"Mummy, Mummy, why are you tho rude to Jarrod?" The sanctuary door closed behind them.

Jarrod looked at Sam. Sam shrugged and broke into

the opening measures of "Immortal, Invisible." The choir took up the verse.

Chapter 5

Aggie came to a halt in the middle of the foyer. She turned and looked at Teddy. "You're an ass too," she said. She turned and continued on her way.

"Mummy!" Teddy's voice held a note of desperation and protest.

"You're just like your father, totally useless." Aggie pushed the outside door open and struggled into the November cold. "The best thing he ever did was die."

"Mummy!" Teddy was on the edge of tears. Aggie let the door go. "Just go back to your service. I'll talk to you in the morning."

Teddy's breath fogged the window of the door. "But Mummy, I thought this was what you wanted." He looked at his mug of coffee with distaste, then took a sip. "Vitamins curdle the milk and coffee's no good cold," he muttered. "I've done everything I could for you, Mummy, and you treat me this way. It's no wonder Daddy left when he did." He turned away from the door and took another mouthful of coffee then wiped his mouth with the sleeve of his suit. He belched softly, then pushed open the door to the sanctuary. The congregation was singing the last stanza of "God leads us along."

Pastor Teddy took a deep breath and walked toward the front of the sanctuary. He tripped on the first step to the dais, righted himself then climbed to the pulpit. He held onto the pulpit with both hands and faced the congregation. He hiccuped and cleared his throat.

"Good evening, everyone, and welcome." Teddy's voice was clear and strong. "My, this is a lovely group we have here this evening." He turned toward Sam. "Isn't it a great group, Pastor Sam?"

"It certainly is," said Sam. "And everyone in such good voice."

"Good voice, my eye," said Molly. Her voice was inaudible to the physical world.

"They got along better after Aggie stomped out," said Lucy.

"Cod liver oil is better without Aggie," said Molly.

She turned her attention to the physical again. "Shh, Teddy's getting ready to give the sermon."

"It's always been a wonder to me how he can preach so clearly when in person he has such a terrible lisp," said Lucy.

"Divine intervention," said Molly. "Now shush."

Teddy sat at his desk staring into the shadows created by his desk lamp. A soft rap sounded at his door and Alberta stuck her head into the room.

"I'm leaving just now, Pastor," she said. "Do you need anything before I go?"

Teddy looked up and stared at Alberta for a moment. Then he said: "You're a blething, Mith Alberta." He turned back to studying the shadows. "A true blething." He sighed.

Alberta blinked. "Why—why, thank you, Pastor. That's the nicest thing you've ever said to me." She started to withdraw then realized Teddy had not replied to her question. "So, is there anything I can do before

I go?"

Teddy sighed again. "Thank you, Mith Alberta. There's not a thing you can do to help me. Thafe home and lock your doorth." He returned to his shadows.

Molly and Lucy sat side by side on the love seat unseen by anyone in the physical. "He's in hard shape this evening," said Lucy.

Molly nodded. "He's in hard shape most of the time. I wonder what Aggie said to him that dropped him into the pits?"

Larry filtered through office wall and sat down in the wing chair. "Aggie told him he was useless," said Larry. He swept off his Gainsborough hat and hung it on his knee. "Now he's questioning everything he's ever done."

"I'd like to wring Aggie's neck," said Lucy. "No matter how ineffectual he is, he didn't deserve that."

"She's a nasty one," said Larry. "I wouldn't mind giving her a haunting too."

Molly sat up straight on the edge of the love seat.

"Oh, do, Larry. It'll be such fun."

"Can't," said Larry. "I have council meetings and a workshop all next week and I don't like to leave when the job is only half done." He stared across the room at Teddy. "You have my permission to do whatever you think is suitable to Aggie, short of killing her. She still has her assignment to complete before she can come over." Larry picked up his hat and put it on his head. He flourished his cape around his shoulders and turned toward the door. "Just harassing her should do the trick. Ta!" His bulky form dissipated through the wall.

Molly looked at Lucy. "That was certainly generous of him. Leaving us to our own devices. That's certainly a step up."

"Don't even think of it!" Larry's voice boomed from the hallway.

Molly rolled her eyes. "I should have known." Larry's presence faded from the air. Molly turned her attention to Pastor Teddy. He sat in his leather office chair and leaned his head against the back. He sniffed hard.

"I should hand him a tissue," said Molly.

"No, don't," said Lucy. "He's crying." She wrinkled her brow. "Whatever Aggie said to him must have been really hurtful."

"Old hag!" said Molly.

"Let's just do something kind for him and leave him alone," said Lucy. She rose from her seat and floated to Teddy's side. She pulled a clean tissue from her sleeve and dabbed at Teddy's wet cheeks. "Don't cry, Teddy, she's not worth it." She stroked Teddy's forehead and hair as if he were a child and the faint odour of her perfume drifted into Teddy's consciousness. He relaxed into his chair and closed his eyes.

"And no more vitamins tonight." Molly peered into the plastic mug. "There's none here to have anyway."

Teddy slept in his armchair until the sun rose the next morning. He awoke to the taste of old coffee and vitamins. His head hurt and he rubbed his face, it was rough with stubble. He sat straight up and winced. Aggie's tirade from the evening before came to his mind.

He winced again at the memory.

I don't know why she does that, he thought.

"She's a frustrated preacher," said Molly in his mind. Pastor Teddy startled and looked around the office. "You can't see me," said Molly, "so don't waste your effort."

I'm having hallucinations, thought Teddy. I wish I had a drink. He stared into the shadows where the sun hadn't quite reached.

"Drink has been your undoing," said Molly. "Just look at yourself. You're under the influence most of the time, you let everyone else do your job for you, and half the time you don't know what's going on. You're just lucky no one but Miss Alberta knows about your 'vitamins.'"

"Mith Alberta knows?" said Teddy aloud. He blinked and looked around the office. He shook his head to clear it. "Now I'm talking to myself. I'm really a mess."

"That you are," said Molly. "If it weren't for her you'd be out of a job, so moaning about it won't do you a bit of good."

Teddy belched and rubbed his stomach. "I suppose not." He sighed and belched again. He opened the bottom drawer of his desk and began rummaging for his vitamins.

"There aren't any," said Molly. "I took them away last night."

"How dare you?" Teddy pulled out the drawer and dumped its contents on the desk. He shuffled through the pile of stained sermon drafts and old notes.

"Save your energy." Molly sat down on the edge of the desk, arranged her royal blue caftan around her knees and then looked at Teddy. "You haven't got any and, believe it or not, you're lucky."

"How can I be lucky without my vitaminth?" He stared around the office once more. "Who are you, anyway?"

"My name is Molly, and you would do well to listen to me."

Teddy shook his head and rubbed at his eyes again.

"Either I'm hallucinating or thith is real," he muttered. "If I'm hallucinating then I'm probably crazy, or there's someone really there who I can't thee. In which case I'm still crazy. Not much choice."

"No, there's not," agreed Molly. She slipped off the edge of the desk and floated over to the sofa and sat down.

"Why don't you show yourthelf?

"It won't do any good, you're not gifted. So brace up and get hold of your life."

"Why should I?" Teddy's voice became more firm and sure. He sat up straight in his chair.

"Look at yourself, man. You're sitting there with a king-sized headache, talking to someone you can't see. You need a bath and a change of clothes and a shave." Molly rose from her place on the love seat. She lifted the mirror off the wall behind the door and carried it across to Teddy's desk and thrust it under his chin. "Just look at yourself."

Teddy shrunk back against his chair. He stared at the mirror.

Molly pushed the mirror under his chin once more. "Look at yourself. Your mother writes your sermons for you and then bullies you into using them."

"H-how d'you know that?" Teddy's chin began to tremble. "I've never told anyone about that."

"I paid her a visit. She drove your father away, and she'll drive you away too, if you don't do something to stop her." Molly set the mirror down. "You realize that Miss Alberta is about the only one on your side."

"She ith?" Teddy's voice rose to a squeak.

"She covers for you all the time. I don't know what you'll do when she retires."

"She's retiring?" Teddy's voice dropped an octave. "How d'you know that?"

"I heard her telling her friend at lunch a couple of weeks ago. As a matter of fact, she said she was just hanging on to get all her retirement plan."

"Why can't I thee you?" Teddy stared wildly around the room. "Why don't you show yourthelf?"

Molly sighed. "Okay, I'll try to manifest. Look at the

love seat, and don't blink because I don't know how long I can stay visible."

Teddy stared at the love seat and tried not to blink. The air around the sofa began to move and darken. Presently the pale form of a middle-aged woman in a royal blue caftan came into hazy focus. "Call me Molly," she said.

Teddy blinked and the vision faded. "Oh, I wish I had thome vitaminth."

"Vitamins won't help. They'll just make it worse. Now, you'd better get a move on and get cleaned up. Miss Alberta will be arriving for work and you don't want her to see you like this."

"Mith Alberta comes in this early?"

"Always," said Molly. "She has a great deal of responsibility. This place would crumble before your eyes if she weren't here."

"Poor Mith Alberta," said Teddy, "I never knew."

"I'm leaving now," said Molly. "Manifesting like that has drained all my energy."

Teddy sat for a few minutes staring at the love seat. I don't believe it. I just don't believe it. Miss Alberta's retiring, and I'm hearing things, and I've made Mummy awfully angry. He picked up the mirror from the desk and looked at his reflection. Molly's right. I do look ill. The incongruity of talking to Molly escaped him for the moment. He sat contemplating the day's growth of beard on his chin and the bags under his eyes. I just look so old. The door to the office slammed and Teddy sat up and listened. That must be Miss Alberta, he thought. I don't want her seeing me looking like this. She's been a loyal employee all these years.

Teddy waited until he heard Alberta rattling the coffee pot. Presently he heard her footsteps fade away down the corridor. She's gone to get water. I'll just slip out while she's gone. He shrugged into his coat and wrapped his scarf around his neck. He pulled on his hat, and slipped out the side door barely missing Alberta. The cold bright sun hurt his eyes and made his head ache. He touched the skin over his sinuses and winced.

I've got to stay away from those vitamins, he thought. He pulled his hat off to ease his aching head but the sunlight made it worse. He put the hat back on and unlocked his car door. He turned the car on then began rummaging in the glove box looking for a spare pint of vitamins. There was none. He felt panic rising in his chest. What am I going to do? They're not open until ten o'clock and it's still only seven-thirty.

Molly slid through the side door and into the passenger seat. "Are you still looking for those vitamins? I heard you, not two sentences ago, renouncing them forever."

"Oh, it'th you again. What difference doeth it make to you?" He pulled his hat down over his eyes and groaned.

"Because you're my assignment and I mean to have it completed before Christmas, and you'd better get to a gas station, you're just about running on fumes." Molly hunched further into her overcoat. "Your car is plenty warm now, and you've got just enough gas to get you to the filling station on the corner. So get moving."

Molly saw Teddy safely to the filling station then went in search of Lucy. She found her coming out of the department store with several packages under her arm. "Hi, Molly. I've just been shopping. They have the prettiest twin sets on sale right now. So much nicer than the ones at home."

Molly frowned. "Shopping? Why do you need to go shopping when you can manifest whatever you want? You're a spirit, anyway."

Lucy hung her head. "Just nostalgia for the life before I transitioned. I so enjoyed trying on clothes."

"I've been looking for you all over, and this is where I find you—shopping."

"I heard you calling but I was in the dressing room trying on things. I was down to my bra and panties." Lucy rearranged the sacks under her arm and buttoned her coat to the top. "It's awfully cold today. What was it you wanted me for?"

Molly shook her head. "We've got a problem on our hands bigger than we thought."

"What's that?" Lucy wandered down the main street window shopping.

"Will you pay attention. It's Teddy. I think he's an alcoholic."

Lucy stopped in the middle of the sidewalk and looked at Molly. "Oh, no!"

Molly nodded. "He'd slept his drunk off by this morning and was quite agitated when he realized he couldn't get anymore until the stores opened."

"Tsk," said Lucy, "we do have our work cut out for us if we want to be home for Christmas. Have you thought of a plan?"

"A major haunting is about as far as we can go." Molly flung her scarf more firmly across her shoulders. "He's on his way home just now."

Lucy frowned. "He stayed at the church all night?"

Molly nodded. "I think it was the first time, since he didn't want Alberta seeing him in that condition. I guess we'll have to put the pressure on and keep it on until he consents to the cure."

Lucy hailed a passing spirit. "Flo, will you take these purchases home for me, please? I have to stay here and help Molly." She handed the packages to Flo and waved good bye.

"Let's go," said Molly. She pulled her turban more closely around her ears. "The sooner we get started on this, the sooner we'll be finished."

Teddy made a wide turn into his driveway barely missing the mail box. He skidded to a stop just short of the garage doors.

Molly and Lucy looked at each other from their seat on the porch swing. "If I didn't know that the stores were still closed, I'd say he's been into the vitamins again," said Molly.

"There's a little corner store just behind the church that opens early, he probably went there." Lucy leaned farther ahead in her seat to better watch Teddy.

"How'd you know that?" Molly sat back and looked at her friend.

"I was out getting the lay of the land the other day and I saw Alberta go there for a box of tissues for the office."

"You are a wonder." Molly looked down the driveway at the car. Teddy had slumped sideways in the seat. "C'mon Lucy, we've got to get him into the house and cleaned up before Mummy sees him." She hitched herself off the swing and floated down the driveway.

Lucy followed. They stood looking into the car at Teddy. "Is he dead?" asked Lucy.

"No, but he will be if he doesn't stay off the vitamins." Molly slipped inside the car and settled herself on the seat next to Teddy. Lucy sat in the back.

"C'mon, Teddy, wakey, wakey." Molly manifested herself and wrested the pint bottle out of his hand.

Teddy groaned. "Leave me alone." He opened his eyes and looked at Molly. "Oh, it's you again. Why don't you just go away."

Molly hid the bottle under her caftan. "Because I wouldn't be doing my duty for you." She began to fade from sight. "I only have a few weeks left."

That's right," said Lucy from the back seat. "We both want to be home for Christmas."

Teddy startled and peered into the shadows of the back seat. "There's two of you ?" He moaned and tried to settle his spinning head by closing his eyes. That made it worse so he opened them again, being careful not to make any sudden moves.

"Yes," said Molly, "and we can call up an army of volunteers if we have to. So, you'd better straighten up and fly right. You're not doing yourself a bit of good, living like this and Mummy is bound to find out. Hurry, or she'll catch you." Molly pushed him until he opened the door.

"Okay, okay." Teddy looked around for his bottle of vitamins.

"Is this what you want?" asked Molly. She held out the bottle.

Teddy grabbed for it and missed. He groaned and held onto his aching head.

Molly put it away again. "Well, you can't have it." She floated out the driver's side door taking the bottle with her. She took the top off and poured it on the ground.

Teddy groaned and eased his plump body out of the car. "Mummy's prize roses! Oh, what she'll do to me."

"Humph," said Molly. "Don't you mean your prize roses? After all, you did do all the work on them."

Teddy sighed. "Yes, but Mummy claims them, and it's just as easy to let her than to get into a wrangle over them." He sighed again.

Molly shook her head. "Poor Teddy, you've never had a chance, have you?"

Teddy let go of his head and sat staring at his hands, back and front. "No, I never have. And what good would it have done if I had?"

Chapter 6

Jarrod stopped by Alberta's desk long enough to drop a list on top of the bulletins she was typing for next weekend's service. "See that invitations get sent to those people, Miss Alberta. Let me see them when you've finished." He turned on his heel and strutted away down the hall.

"Please, Miss Alberta," muttered Alberta staring down the hall after Jarrod.

"And thank you, Miss Alberta," said Sam.

"I don't think those two words are in his vocabulary." Alberta picked up the list and scanned it. "Goodness, he wants everyone here except the Pope."

Sam laughed. "And why would he invite the Pope?"

Alberta shrugged. "Who knows. Maybe he wants to convert him." She scanned down the list again. "I'll make one version and show that to him. If he's satisfied, I'll copy them."

Sam held out another list. "When you're finished

with that I'd like you to order these choral parts. Be sure and get a copy of the orchestration for Miss Jo." Sam's eyes twinkled. "Please, and thank you, Miss Alberta."

"Certainly, Pastor Sam." Alberta smiled back at him.

The outer door opened and let in a gust of winter air. it slammed shut a moment later. "That must be Pastor Teddy. He's late this morning." Alberta rose to greet Teddy.

"Good morning, Mith Alberta. I'm glad to see you this morning." Teddy rubbed at his freshly shaven chin and peeled off the bits of toilet paper he had used to control the bleeding.

"You need a styptic pencil, Pastor."

Teddy waved the suggestion away. "I'll get one on the way home, thank you, Mith Alberta." He turned toward his office. He turned back to Alberta. "Can you give me an update on the Christmath Pageant? A cup of coffee would be welcome, too. Thank you, Mith Alberta." He turned and entered his office.

Alberta raised her bushy gray eyebrows and looked

after Teddy. "Oh, my heart, two thank yous in one morning, and it's only just after nine."

Sam chuckled. "I hope it's not more than you can stand." He turned and walked toward his office. "Oh, by the way, can you get me Miss Ridgeway's phone number, please. No hurry with either thing." He opened his office door.

"Hm," said Alberta. "So he wants Jane's phone number. Wouldn't it be wonderful if ..." Alberta thrust the thought out of her mind and shook her head. "I'm too old to be matchmaking."

The outside door slammed and Maggie appeared around the comer with several packages under her arms. She tried to elbow her way through the door to the office but only succeeded in dropping most of her armload on the floor. "Drat!" she muttered, then bent to pick them up.

Alberta rose and held the door for her. "You've been shopping?"

"Again," said Maggie. She dropped her packages onto the stacking chair that served in the reception area. "I hope this is the last time."

"D'you mean this is not the first time?" Alberta picked up one of the bags and peered into it. "You're going gaudy this year?"

"I wish. This is for the Christmas pageant." Maggie unbuttoned her coat and hung it on the coat rack.

Alberta's eyebrows rose a fraction. "Jarrod's been at it again?"

"And again and again and again." Maggie rolled her eyes. "Is the coffee hot? I'm nearly frozen." She inspected a mug for debris, then held it under the spigot. "I went out as soon as the stores opened this morning. Almost all the glittery stuff is gone." She sipped at her coffee. "Are you going to the meeting at Lizzie's this evening?"

"Definitely," said Alberta. She warmed her hands on her own mug of coffee. "I need to know when to duck out of sight. So what has Jarrod been doing that has you out shopping at this late date? There's not much time left before pageant."

Maggie sighed. "I know. He changed the costumes in the magi scene."

"Weren't they gaudy enough for him? You had all those costumes done and fitted hadn't you?"

Maggie nodded. "I thought I was finished with those and all I had left to do was the innkeeper and his wife. I wouldn't be this far along with them if Barbara Ann hadn't come by all week to help me with the finishing touches." She sipped her coffee.

"I didn't know Barbara Ann could sew."

"She's actually a pretty good seamstress. The woman who runs the workshop where she goes every day taught them how. She even taught the men. In fact, Barbara Ann has a very good eye for fabric and can create the proper drape and produce it." Maggie fell silent. Presently she said: "I hope this is the last shopping trip I'll have to make."

The outer door opened and a rush of cold air blew

in under the office door. Soon the thump and click of Aggie's walker could be heard. Alberta rose to assist her with the inside door. "Good day, Aggie."

"A good day my foot," said Aggie. "How can it be a good day when the weather is this cold and people don't shovel their walks?" She began struggling out of her coat. "Help me." She began to lose her balance and grabbed for her walker. Maggie rose quickly to keep her from falling over. Aggie righted herself and peered through the steam on her glasses at Maggie.

"You're here too. I might have known. Nothing to do but sit and drink coffee with your friends all morning, Miss Alberta?"

Maggie shook her head behind Aggie's back, then said: "Actually not, Miss Aggie. I was on an errand for Pastor Jarrod that required me to come by, and I was so cold when I got here Alberta offered me a cup to warm up."

Aggie turned her head to the side and peered up at Alberta. "So what's your excuse?"

"I didn't think I needed one," said Alberta. "It is, after all, my office."

"And your coffee too, I suppose." Aggie hobbled toward Teddy's office. "Is Teddy in?"

"As a matter of fact, he's out doing pastoral visits this morning." Alberta lied with a straight face.

Aggie turned around and made her painful way back to the reception area. "You mean, out visiting all the eligible widows." Aggie sniffed. "They couldn't catch him when they were in their prime, I don't know why they think they'll be able to catch him now." She began struggling into her coat again.

"Actually, he went to the nursing home," said Alberta. "There are several of our elderly members who can't get out to service any more."

Aggie snorted. "I hope he doesn't get any ideas going there. Annie Sykes was never one to waste words when she had something on her mind. She'd tell the truth and shame the devil." She finished buttoning her coat. "Tell Teddy I was here." She wrestled with the office door until Maggie held it open for her. Presently the outer door banged.

Maggie made a face. "She's twisted. She has to be twisted. Mrs. Sykes is pushing a hundred." She drained her coffee mug and stood up. "I must keep on going, I have some shopping of my own to do. I'll see you this evening at Lizzie's."

Alberta climbed the last few steps to Lizzie's front door and rang the bell. Jane opened the front door just as Alberta reached to ring the bell again.

"Hi there, Alberta. We're all in the kitchen. Let me take your tray for you."

"Thank you, Jane. I'll just hang up my coat and be right with you." Alberta hung her coat on the hook and entered the kitchen. It was warm, and smelled of nutmeg and freshly ground coffee.

"Good evening ladies. I see we're all here. I'm sorry to be late. I just now got finished at the office."

"Just now?" Maggie's voice rose in her disbelief.

Alberta nodded. "I finished the bulletins and got them printed and just as I was going out the door, Jarrod came by with another list that had to be done five minutes ago." She pulled out a kitchen chair and settled herself at the table.

"He thinks he's pretty hot stuff," said Barbara Ann.

Alberta blinked. "I didn't know you were going to be here this evening, Barbara Ann. How'd you know we were meeting?"

"She came to visit with me this afternoon and stayed to supper," said Lizzie. "Don't worry, she knows how necessary it is to keep quiet about this."

"Are you sure?" Alberta wrinkled her brow as she looked across the table at Barbara Ann.

"Of course, I do," said Barbara Ann. "I may be slow, but I'm not totally stupid. I won't tell a soul." She leaned her elbows on the edge of the table. "Actually, I think it's time that Jarrod got his comeuppance, and I know that you can't be seen as a trouble-maker." She paused for breath. "I feel a little bad about doing that to Pastor

Waters. He has always been nice to me."

Alberta reached across the table and patted Barbara Ann's arm. "Of course you do, so do we. But you know that in order to get to Jarrod and a few of the others we have to take our opportunities when they come around."

"What goes around, comes around," said Barbara Ann.

"Now, hon," said Lizzie, "it's Jarrod's turn to get his, and we're not going to hurt him, just frustrate him."

Barbara Ann took this in and then sighed. "If only Jarrod could at least be polite."

"He can't," said Jane, "and every one of us knows it."

Lizzie began pouring coffee and handed the full cups to Jane. Barbara Ann pulled the plastic wrap off the tray that Alberta had brought. "Oh, goody, chocolate chips! My favourite." She passed the tray to everyone, then took one herself.

"Pass those my way," said Mollie from her unseen perch on the edge of the counter.

"Me too," said Lucy. She hitched herself onto the

edge of the sink beside Molly.

"I do like meetings where they serve chocolate chip cookies," said Molly.

"I guess I'd better call I the meeting to order," said Maggie. "Does anyone have any old business?" She glanced around the table. "No? Does anyone have any new business?"

"I have a question," said Jane. "How do we get the word out to the other ladies in the congregation?"

"I've been thinking about that," said Sandra. "Suppose when we choose the time to pull this off we call all the women who volunteer their time one way or the other and set up a phony meeting that Pastor Teddy calls."

"Why would Pastor Teddy call a phony meeting?" asked Barbara Ann.

"He won't, we will," said Jane. "I think the time to act is on the evening of the Christmas pageant. That'll have the most impact on them."

"But that's kind of mean." said Barbara Ann. "After

all, the others have worked hard putting this together. Just look at Miss Maggie, she's done all the sewing for this."

"And I really appreciated your help," said Maggie. "I couldn't have gotten finished in time without you."

Barbara Ann's cheeks reddened at the compliment. "I was proud to help," she said. She turned to Maggie. "Aren't you sorry to do all that work and then not be able to use it?"

"No, I'm not. It's for the greater good of the women in this congregation, and we have to strike at the most inconvenient time for Jarrod. Besides, we can use the costumes next year."

"Oh," said Barbara Ann. She thought it over for a moment then said: "I still think it's mean."

Alberta sighed. "Of course, it is, Barbara Ann. That's why it'll work. Jarrod has been more than mean to every woman in the congregation and he needs to be shown the error of his ways."

"We'll have to make a list," said Sandra.

"I can help you with that," said Alberta. "The Sunday school list is up to date, I'll just make a copy of that."

"I have access to the choir roster," said Jane.

"I can get the roll for the hospitality committee," said Sandra.

"I can make a copy of the Bible study classes," said Barbara Ann. "I deliver them to all the classes after service. I thought you said we were being mean? I thought it over again, and I saw how we can't let it go on. There have been too many hurt feelings."

"How d'you know that?" asked Jane.

"People tell me things. I may be slow, but I've got a pair of ears," said Barbara Ann.

"That's right," said Alberta. "Barbara Ann has a very sympathetic ear and a lot of good sense."

Barbara Ann ducked her head. "Thank you, Miss Alberta. I enjoy being able to serve."

"We need to get back to the subject," said Jane. "Once we get all these lists together we'll divide them up between ourselves and call every woman on them."

"Everyone except Aggie," said Sandra. "If she gets wind of it, we'll all be in the soup."

"We can't do anything until the last minute," said Lizzie. "We risk being discovered if we do it too soon."

"Is there anyone in the church that we can depend on to share the list and keep quiet about it? It's a lot of phoning if we keep it to ourselves."

"There's old Grannie Banks, and Mrs. Doniphan," said Alberta. "They're reliable, and I know for a fact they're both fed up with the situation."

"They're safe as a bank when it comes to a confidence." Lizzie rose to pour more coffee. "I knew them when they were young and they were solid like that even then, and they've been friends for fifty years."

"We'll have to synchronize the lists so we won't be calling anyone twice," said Alberta.

Jane reached for another cookie. "We need to talk to all the women who are in the play. Of all the people who shouldn't be there, they're the most important."

"They're probably good and fed up with Jarrod by

now," said Sandra. "They've been suffering under his control these past two months."

"What about the young girls who are in the congregation?" Barbara Ann reached for the last cookie.

"What about them?" asked Jane.

"Do we include them in this strike?"

Jane looked around at the others. "What about it?"

"I think, just the ones in the play or working behind the scenes," said Lizzie. "The fewer people who know what's going on, the less likely the plan will be uncovered."

"Some of those girls have a major crush on Jarrod and they'd likely tell him," said Alberta.

"That's all the more reason to exclude them," said Jane. She closed her notebook. "Get the lists as soon as you can and give them to Alberta. She and I can do the collating of names. We'll meet again when that's ready."

"What do you think I should wear when I get baptized?" said Barbara Ann. "Should I have my hair done for it?"

"You don't have to worry about that. Your clothes will be just as wet, new or old," said Alberta. "As for your hair, it's fine the way it is and it'll be just as wet as your clothes. Anyway, It's not about appearances. It's about faith in the risen Saviour. He told us not to worry about what we will eat or what we will put on, so you just have to step out in faith. Can you do that?"

"I think so." Barbara Ann fidgeted with the button on her coat. "That's what they were talking about in the class I took these past few weeks. Pastor Waters led it." The button that she was fiddling with came off in her hand. "D'you know, Miss Alberta, I never noticed before that Pastor Waters has a terrible lisp."

"That has been the bane of his existence all his life," said Alberta. "He was teased mercilessly when he was in school."

"He wears strong aftershave too."

Alberta looked up at Barbara Ann. "He does? I've never noticed. When was this?" She paid close attention to Barbara Ann.

"During class." Barbara Ann made a top of her button and began spinning it on the edge of the desk. "I noticed it as soon as he closed the door. The youngsters in the class were talking about it."

"Were they?" Alberta cocked her head. "Perhaps I should drop him a hint that he's using too much."

Barbara Ann blinked. "If you think it's a good thing to do. I wouldn't like him to know that it was me complaining. I like him. He has always been kind to me." Barbara Ann's button spun its way off the desk.

"I won't mention you at all."

"It gets quite strong when we're in a closed room with him, and the room we were using is small." Barbara Ann retrieved her button from under the work table.

"I'll see to it," said Alberta. "I need some help collating these lists. D'you have time?"

"I quit!" said Laurie. "Nothing I do pleases you." She jumped off the stage and slapped her copy of the script on the table.

Jarrod jumped out of his seat. "Now Laurie, you can't do that. Who'll play Mary at this late date?"

"That's not my concern and I don't care." Laurie turned away and stomped toward the door.

"Outspoken little witch," muttered Jarrod. "You were like this since the day you were born. You cried all through the baby dedication."

The door slammed behind Laurie. Jarrod hastened after her.

"Laurie, wait up a moment, dear." Jarrod's voice choked on the dear.

Laurie kept on walking. Jarrod caught up to her and grabbed her arm. Laurie pulled herself from his grasp.

"Don't you put your hands on me!" She began to walk toward the office. Jarrod walked beside her.

"Now, Laurie, be reasonable. Who can I get to play Mary at this late date?"

"Miss Maggie wanted to play that part." Laurie suppressed a smile at Jarrod's horrified face.

"No, no. Miss Maggie's too old. She's too fat."

Laurie shrugged. "Will you be decent to me and the others from now on?"

Jarrod's jaw muscles worked overtime while he considered this offer. His shoulders slumped. "I'll treat you all with the utmost respect." His tone took on an element of sarcasm. Laurie narrowed her eyes at him. "What's that you said?"

"I'm sorry and I'll treat you all reasonably."

Laurie pursed her lips as if considering his promise.

"Okay, but you promised."

"You drive a hard bargain, Miss Laurie."

"So does my mother."

Molly and Lucy convened on top of the file cabinet next to Alberta's desk. "Wow!" said Molly. "She fights like a grownup."

"She has always been feisty, even as a child. Her mother's like that too."

"I think Alberta may have another ally. Laurie is a ring leader among the other teens."

"How'll Miss Alberta even know about it?" asked Lucy.

"I'll put a bug in Pastor Teddy's ear," replied Molly. "He and I are developing a close relationship. He can tell Miss Alberta about it."

Lucy turned toward Molly, nearly losing her seat on the file cabinet. "Have you been manifesting to him?"

"Once."

Lucy righted herself. "How come you never told me?"

"It was only once and I forgot about it as soon as it was over."

"I don't see why I should miss all the fun. How'd he take it?"

"He came around quickly to our point of view once I proved to him he wasn't hallucinating."

Lucy clucked her tongue. "You're naughty. Can I come too?"

"Of course." Molly floated off the top of the file cabinet. "He's in his office working on his sermon just now. He's been refreshing himself with his vitamins."

"D'you mean that seeing you wasn't enough to make

him quit?" Lucy wafted down the hall after Molly.

"I'm not that ugly, Lucy." She filtered through the wall into Pastor Teddy's office. Lucy followed. They arranged themselves on either side of Teddy and looked over his shoulder. He was indeed working on a sermon. His coffee cup was half empty.

Molly exerted her astral strength and tipped the mug over. Coffee ran everywhere.

"Drat!" said Teddy. He grabbed a handful of tissues and began mopping up the mess.

"Getting sloppy in our old age, are we?" sang Molly in his right ear.

Teddy stopped mopping and listened. He heard nothing. He set the cup upright and began mopping again.

Molly gave an astral push and tipped the coffee mug over once more. "Speak when you're spoken to, Teddy."

Teddy peered into the afternoon shadows but saw nothing. "It's you again. What d'you want?"

"We have a problem."

Teddy groaned. "So now it's we. Who's the other

part of the we?"

"Lucy's with me, but I was referring to you and me."

"So why do we have a problem?"

"Pastor Jarrod is alienating the cast of the Christmas pageant. Miss Alberta needs to know that."

"Why?" Teddy sat down on his chair and lobbed the wad of soggy tissues in the direction of the waste can. It was a basket.

"Hey, you're good," said Molly.

"I used to play basketball in high school. As a matter of fact, a couple of the college recruiters offered me a scholarship to their schools."

"And did you take it?"

Teddy sagged back into his chair. "No. Mummy wouldn't let me." He leaned his chin on the palm of his hand. "She would never let me do anything I really liked."

"That's too bad."

"I wath good those dayth." Teddy stared into the distance of the past and smiled.

"Well, no use crying over spilled milk," said Molly. "We have an assignment for you. Listen up. You must do something about Pastor Jarrod or there'll be no Christmas Pageant." Molly outlined the problem to Teddy. "You need to let Jarrod know that he can't treat anyone this way, especially the girls, in particular, Miss Laurie."

Teddy groaned. "Do I have to?" He searched for his cup of coffee, then remembered he'd spilled it. "The last time I thaid anything to him about appropriate behaviour, he tattled it all over the congregation and made me look like a total fool. That wath just after he came here, and I know no one hath ever forgotten."

"How'd you know that?" asked Molly. She unfolded her arms and floated over to the wing chair and sat down.

"Becauth I heard him do it, and to this day, he goes out of his way to remind me." Teddy stared down at his hands, looking at first the back and then the front of each one.

"You should have stopped the behaviour immediately. Why didn't you?" Molly arranged her caftan more smoothly around her knees and then crossed them.

"I would have, except Mummy happened by just then and she liketh Jarrod. It wath before her arthritis made her have to use a walker. She would come around any-time she felt like it, and I never knew when she'd come or what kind of mood she'd be in when she got here. She and Jarrod were as thick as thieves for a long time, and there wathn't a thing I could do about it." Teddy sighed. "And you think I can change either one of them."

"I think you can," said Molly, "but you'll have to change yourself first." She watched the thoughts flicker across Teddy's face.

"Change how?" said Teddy. "I'm no match even for Mummy, supposing I did change. How could I possibly make Jarrod change?" Teddy picked up his coffee cup again and discovered it still empty. He sighed and set it back down.

"First of all," said Molly, "you've got to get dried out. You can't continue in your present path and expect to have any respect from anyone. People will soon be noticing and that would be too bad, considering all the grief you've suffered to get here."

"How can I get dried out without people knowing about it?"

Molly sighed and shook her head. "Use your imagination, get creative. You're a big boy now. You've got a problem and you're the only one who can fix it. What's that expression the kids are using these days? Get with the program."

Teddy groaned and clutched at his aching head.

"Mummy'th not going to like this."

Molly stamped her foot soundlessly. "Who cares what Mummy likes? She has never put herself out for you, why should you care?

Teddy shrugged. "Habit, I guess." He crossed his arms on the desk and buried his head in them.

"Not a good one." Molly firmed up her lips. "You deserve to be better treated, but unless you take the bull by the horns and make people pay attention it will never happen."

Chapter 7

"Mith Alberta, I'm going to be away for a few dayth. I want you to hold the fort while I'm gone." Teddy's normally ruddy cheeks flushed even more.

Alberta raised her shaggy eyebrows. "May I ask where you 're going?"

"No, you may not. If Mummy comes by while I'm gone just tell her I'm out doing pastoral visits."

"So even Miss Aggie doesn't know you're going?"

"Especially not her." Teddy's cheeks reddened again and he looked down and began fiddling with a loose button on his coat. "I planned it all from here so I wouldn't have tell her." He drew a deep breath and turned away from Alberta, then turned toward her again. "If you run out of excuses you can make one up. I'll back whatever you thay."

"Who's going to preach this weekend?" Alberta picked up a piece of scrap paper and began folding it smaller and smaller. She threw the paper down and looked up at Teddy through her thick eyebrows.

"I've left a message with Jarrod. If he wanth the pulpit badly enough, and I know he doeth, he'll grab at the chance."

Teddy turned away from Alberta. "I'm leaving in a few minutes, so if you have any questions before I go, make it snappy."

Alberta watched Teddy wend his way down the hall. He bumped into his door post as he always did and presently she heard a discreet belch as she always did. I wonder what's up with him, she thought. He was uncommonly decisive today. She sat watching for his departure but he merely waved at her and went out the back door. "Hm!" Alberta frowned. "Hm!"

"What are you 'hming' about?" asked Jane.

Alberta startled and put her hand on her chest to still her racing heart. "Oh, Jane, it's you. What're you doing here in the middle of the afternoon?"

"I finished my classes for the day and I thought I'd stop by to see how things were going." Jane unbuttoned her coat and pulled her scarf away from her throat.

"Between you and me?" Alberta studied Jane's expression.

"Always," said Jane. She settled herself on the moulded chair closest to Alberta's desk and returned Alberta's steady gaze. "So, what's up?"

Alberta pursed her lips. "I'm not sure. Pastor Teddy's acting very strange. I can't figure it out." She shook her head.

"Strange how?"

"Oh, I don't know." Alberta frowned. "He just arrived at my desk a few minutes ago and announced that he was going to be out of town for a few days. Then just before you came in, I saw him going out the back door with his briefcase. He hardly ever carries his briefcase."

"I wonder what's up with him." Jane folded her scarf in a triangle like a flag. "Who's going to preach?"

"He said he'd left a note for Jarrod."

Jane grunted a laugh. "That'll please Jarrod no end."

"I thought so too. And Teddy apparently knows how

Jarrod's been salivating after the pulpit."

Jane began unfolding her scarf. "He has more on the ball than we give him credit for."

"Teddy?"

"Yes. I didn't know Jarrod was so transparent."

"He has made no secret of it."

"Times are getting interesting on the plantation." Jane folded her scarf once more. "When's he due back?"

"He didn't say, but it'll have to be before Christmas Eve because he's doing the communion with the newly baptized."

"D'you mean he didn't delegate that too?"

"Not as far as I know."

A draft of cold air rattled the office door. Presently the click and thump of Aggie's walker announced her arrival. "Where's Teddy?" She let herself down with a grunt onto a plastic chair. She struggled out of her coat. "So where's Teddy?"

Jane and Alberta exchanged glances.

"He just left," said Alberta.

"Where's he gone? I suppose to the nursing home to visit with that Annie Sykes again." Aggie twisted her mouth into a grimace of disapproval.

Alberta shook her head. "I don't think so. He visited her the other day."

"Surely you know where he is." Aggie's cheeks flushed darkly. "Well? You are, after all, his secretary."

Alberta stood and walked to the door. "I am, but that doesn't mean that he has to give me a schedule of his day's activities every time he comes through the door." She held the door open for Aggie and her walker. "He said he wouldn't be back for awhile."

Aggie struggled to her feet. "Are you throwing me out?"

"No," said Alberta. "I'm just making it easier for you."

"Oh!" Aggie shrugged herself back into her coat and jammed her winter hat down over her ears. "This is not the last of this, you mark my words." She turned and made faster progress out the door than when she came in. Presently the outer door slammed shut.

Jane and Alberta looked at each other then began to laugh. "I don't know how you put up with this every day. She's awful."

"Sometimes she misses a day," said Alberta. She laughed hard and mopped at her streaming eyes with a tissue. "It's Teddy I worry about. After all, he has to live with her." Alberta sniffed.

"Can you imagine what kind of mother-in-law she would have made?"

"So Pastor Teddy's on vacation," said Jarrod. He smirked down at Alberta. "D'you know where he went?"

"I have no idea where he's gone or when he'll be back." Alberta began tidying the rosters from the women's Sunday schools and prayer groups. "He didn't confide in me."

"Maybe he'll come back married. Wouldn't that be a hoot?"

Alberta shivered. "I doubt that he will if he hasn't done it before."

Jarrod wagged a finger at Alberta. "You never know. I think he's getting desperate." He dropped the sheets of paper he had been holding onto the pile of rosters on Alberta's desk. "Five copies collated by noon, Miss Alberta."

"Five copies collated by noon." Alberta mouthed the words at Jarrod's retreating back. The sooner we put our plan into motion, the sooner we can get back at him. Forgive me, Father, Jarrod has just gotten on my last nerve.

A gust of arctic air announced the arrival of Barbara Ann. Presently she pushed open the office door. "Guess what, Miss Alberta?"

"Something that has you all excited, I can see. Help yourself to the coffee and warm up. It's fresh."

"I gotta tell you this first."

Alberta rose and poured two cups of coffee and gave one to Barbara Ann. "So. What's your big news?"

"Pastor Jarrod asked me to be one of the angels in the Christmas pageant. I get to fly over the heads of the audience and sing with the choir. It'll be just like bungee jumping only safer."

"I see." Alberta was silent for a moment. Then she asked: "Where are you going to be swinging from?"

"Pastor Jarrod has that all figured out. He's going to have a platform suspended from the rafters and we jump off that. Isn't that exciting?"

Alberta closed her eyes on the image of simple Barbara Ann soaring over the heads of the congregation with only one of Jarrod's ropes between her and mortal danger.

"Miss Alberta?" Barbara Ann's voice seemed to come from very far away. "Miss Alberta? Are you okay?"

Alberta took a deep breath and opened her eyes. "I'm fine, but you may not be for very long. Whose idea was that, yours or Pastor Jarrod's?"

"Pastor Jarrod's. He called me at home and was so very nice and polite to me I could hardly believe it was him. Things are getting better already and I'm not even baptized." Barbara Ann could contain herself no longer.

She threw off her coat and did a little dance to her own music. "I'm so thrilled."

Alberta managed a smile and a little enthusiasm. "I'm glad for you, Barbara Ann, but just take care not to get hurt. We'd miss you if anything happened."

"Laurie! I didn't mean it that way." Pastor Jarrod's voice rose to the pitch of a first alto.

"That's what you said the last time," said Laurie and tossed the wrinkled manuscript onto the table. "C'mon girls. It's the last time he'll use us this way." She turned toward the door.

"But Laurie," said Betsy. "We want to be in the pageant. We don't want to quit."

Several of the other girls murmured between themselves. After a few moments Julie spoke up. "Laurie, we feel that we can't let Pastor Jarrod down this way. After all, Christmas Eve is only a few weeks away."

"Suit yourselves," said Laurie, "but I'm not staying."Laurie went out and closed the door gently behind herself. It will be harder on Pastor Jarrod's nerves if I don't slam it, she thought. Her lips curved into tight smile. I'll slam the outer door instead. She turned toward the coat racks and nearly bumped into Alberta returning to her office with her arms loaded with paper. Everyone was working overtime to produce the Christmas pageant, including the high school seniors who were sacrificing precious study time to participate in the evenings.

"Oops," said Alberta. She grabbed at her bundles of paper in time to prevent a slide.

"You're certainly in a mood today."

Laurie made a face. "I'm always in a mood when Pastor Jarrod is concerned. Why can't he learn to at least be civil?" She pulled her coat and scarf off the hanger and shrugged into them.

Alberta bushy eyebrows rose a fraction, her eyes took on an alert sparkle as she studied Laurie's flushed face. "What did he do this time?"

"The usual boys-are-better-than-girls routine." Laurie's voice lost a little of its anger. She held the office door for Alberta. "That man must have been born on a desert island the way he treats women."

Alberta dropped her stack of letters onto her desk and sat down in her chair. "So what's your response to that?"

Laurie twisted her lips into an apologetic pucker. "I quit for the second time." She dropped down into one of the plastic chairs.

"For the second time," said Alberta. She watched Laurie's expressions come and go. "When was the first time?"

"Two weeks ago. He promised he'd treat the girls with more respect, and it's been downhill ever since."

"So it's not yourself you're defending."

"No. I have this passion for defending everyone."

"Coffee?" Alberta rose and pulled two cups off the spire of Styrofoam standing on the coffee tray. "It's fresh."

"Thanks, but put lots of milk in it." Laurie slid down

into the chair and closed her eyes. "I should be a lawyer for women's issues."

"Yes, you should," said Alberta. She emptied two servings of nondairy creamer into Laurie's cup. "Sugar?"

"No, thanks. I'm watching my diet."

Alberta looked over at Laurie's slender form. "You don't have to diet. You're plenty slender now." She handed the cup of coffee to Laurie.

Laurie sat up and rolled her shoulders. "Yes, now I am, but if I expect to stay this way for the rest of my life, it's something I have to keep working on." She sipped at her coffee.

Alberta settled herself at her desk and looked over at Laurie. "So what did you say to Pastor Jarrod?"

"I quit."

"Just like that?" Alberta set her coffee cup down.

"Weren't you playing Mary?"

Laurie grinned lopsidedly. "I sure was. He'll see how much he depends on women to do all the chores he doesn't want to do. I wish there was some way I could point that out to him a little more forcefully." She sipped at her coffee again.

Alberta picked up a paper clip and began straightening it. "Maybe there is."

"What do you mean?"

"Can you keep a secret?"

"Yeah, I think so."

"I have to know so before I tell you this." The paper clip broke and stuck Alberta's hand before dropping onto the desk. She shook her hand. "So, can I trust you?"

Laurie nodded.

"There are some of us women who have a plan, but we need total secrecy until it's time to put it into motion."

"Oh?" Laurie sat up straighter in her chair.

"Yes, and we can use your help, if you care to give it." Alberta looked across the desk at Laurie.

"What in the world are you up to? Does Mom know?"

"Yes, she knows. But you are never to discuss it with her at home. Can you do that?"

Laurie blinked. "I suppose so. I can't agree to something I don't know about."

"I really shouldn't be telling you here either. You never know who can hear you here."

Laurie wiggled her tidy brown eyebrows at Alberta. "The walls, they have ears."

"No kidding." Alberta lowered her voice. "Here's what we're planning." She told the pertinent facts to Laurie.

Laurie's sherry-brown eyes grew rounder as she took in the audacity of the plan. When Alberta got to the end of the story, Laurie clapped her hands together and she laughed. "Can I play too?"

"Actually you can." Alberta drained the last of the coffee out of her mug. "I know you're influential with the other girls. What I need for you to do is to go back and apologize to Jarrod and make some excuse for quitting and ask for your role back again."

Laurie made a face. "Apologize to Pastor Jarrod?"

"Yes. You may be our only pipeline, so to speak, to the other girls. I need for you to keep me posted as to the atmosphere during rehearsal."

"You want me to be a mole." Laurie's eyes sparkled with mischief. "I could agitate a little behind the scenes and keep the pot of intrigue boiling. Fun!"

Alberta held up a cautioning finger. "Not too much though. This has to be concealed until the last moment."

"Can I talk to Mom about it at all?"

"Only if your father's not around."

Laurie set her half empty cup on the edge of Alberta's desk. "I'll get on it right away." She gathered her coat and scarf into a bundle and went out the door. Presently the soft whoosh of the sanctuary doors alerted Jarrod to her presence.

Jarrod turned his head. "Back so soon?"

Laurie clamped her teeth shut tight. "I've thought it over, and it seems a rather difficult situation I've placed you in at the last minute." She dumped her coat and scarf onto one of the pews. She reached out to pick up the script.

"What makes you think you're welcome?" Jarrod

looked up at Laurie and smirked, his pale freckles coalesced into one beige birthmark.

Laurie looked down at the dialogue in her hands.

"Because you need me." She looked at the script more closely. "This isn't even my script." She rifled through the pages and frowned.

"Of course, it's not." Jarrod's grin grew wider as he enjoyed his moment. "I've given your part to Janie and dropped her part altogether. I can't have a divisive force spoiling my pageant."

Laurie looked over at Janie. Janie dropped her gaze from Laurie's silent question. Laurie allowed tears to gather in her eyes. She looked back at Jarrod and let one of the tears overflow her eyelids and fall onto the back of Jarrod' s hand. It splashed onto the master copy of the play, blurring a few of the opening words.

Jarrod grunted and brushed at the wet spots making the smear worse.

Laurie sniffed hard and allowed a few more tears to roll down her cheeks. She scrubbed at them with a crumpled tissue.

"Oh, Laurie, you can have your part back," said Janie. She jumped off the stage and handed Laurie's script back to her. "I can't keep this from you; it's yours. Take it." She picked up her original script and scrambled back onto the platform.

Laurie squeezed out a few more tears and looked up at Jarrod through her lashes. She sniffed again. "Please, Pastor Jarrod, can I have my part back?"

"Yes, but I don't want to hear one more word about quitting. Is that clear?"

Laurie nodded and smiled a watery smile. "Yes, Pastor Jarrod."

Alberta gathered her stack of rosters together and stuffed them into her brief case. "I'll have to hustle if I'm to get Jarrod's typing done for him," she muttered. "I'm surprised he hasn't been back looking for them."

"Looking for what?" asked Sam.

Alberta pursed her lips. "Pastor Jarrod gave me

some typing and photocopying he wanted done five minutes ago."

Sam's eyes crinkled into his smile. "I'd say he's out of luck, then." He laid a page of music on the desk. "I'll be needing thirty copies of this on Wednesday, please, Miss Alberta. If you don't have time, I can always do it myself, though I always seem to make the machine malfunction when I use it."

"Please don't do that. You really don't have to, I don't mind doing copying for you." Alberta sighed. "All I'd need now for a total collapse of the system would be not getting Jarrod's work typed and copied."

"Late afternoon tomorrow is fine for my work. It's for choir practice."

Alberta picked up the sheet of music. "Is this a new hymn? It's kind of short and repetitive."

Sam nodded. "That's the nature of the music. It's a praise chorus. They're becoming more and more popular these days. I thought they'd make a nice change for the welcome."

"Did you run this by Pastor Teddy?" Alberta studied the words. "I don't know if he'll like this. It's quite out of character from our usual fare." She laid the paper down on her desk once more then looked up at Sam.

"Teddy said it was fine, but I'm not sure he took it in."

Alberta drew her lips into a thin line. "More to the point, what'll Aggie have to say about it?"

Sam's face crinkled into a smile again. "It'll be all over and done with before she can say anything."

The office door flew open and banged against the door stop pushing it farther into the wall. Jarrod pushed through the door. "Have you finished that typing and copying I gave you?"

"I've completed the first three pages. I have one left to go." Alberta made her expression remain neutral and handed the finished pages to Jarrod. "You might want to proofread it before I copy it." She sat down at her desk and began typing.

"Late tomorrow is fine," said Sam. He closed the door

softly behind himself.

"I want these before then," said Jarrod. "You've got a million mistakes here, Miss Alberta. You're going to have to retype at least two of these." He handed the pages back to Alberta.

Alberta scanned the pages. "I don't see anything wrong. Where are these mistakes?"

"'Convenient' is misspelled, and so is 'conference.'" Jarrod pointed out her errors.

Alberta picked up her dictionary and leafed through it. She underlined 'convenient,' then looked at Jarrod's original and underlined the word there too. She handed both the page in question and the dictionary to Jarrod. "I believe the dictionary doesn't lie, Pastor Jarrod." She retrieved the dictionary from Jarrod's freckled hands and looked up 'conference." She handed the dictionary back to Jarrod. "I think this says it all."

Jarrod shrugged and turned away. "I never was very good in spelling,"

Alberta rolled her eyes and turned back to her typing.

It sure feels strange with Pastor Teddy gone. I hope he's okay, thought Alberta. She shrugged and began proofing Jarrod's work. I wonder where in the world he went. She forced her attention back to her task. She deleted several letters from an obscure word, then saved her work.

A gust of cold air rattled the office door. It was a few days later, and Alberta had just started work. Aggie elbowed her way into the office.

"What're you staring for, Alberta?" The office door slammed behind her.

"I'm just surprised to see you, that's all," said Alberta.

"Why? Don't I have a right to be here?" Aggie opened her coat and pulled her gloves off.

"Have you heard from Pastor Teddy yet?"

"Of course not, or I wouldn't be here in this weather." She stomped the residue of snow from her boots. "I don't suppose you have."

Alberta looked down and watched the snow melting under Aggie's feet. "No, I haven't, Aggie, but one of us should hear from him soon. Can I get you some coffee?"

"Half a cup, black, no sugar."

Just as if I were the maid, thought Alberta. She turned toward the coffee urn. "He never even gave you a clue?"

"No. He just disappeared."

Alberta was startled to see tears build up in Aggie's eyes and overflow down her cheeks. She handed Aggie the box of tissues.

"I'm so worried about him. He hasn't been himself these past few months." Aggie sniffed and dabbed at her eyes with a tissue. "I've caught him talking to himself more than once, and once he stayed out all night. I didn't know where he was."

Alberta frowned. "I didn't think he'd taken to staying out all night."

"Just once." Aggie stared hard at Alberta. "Now you're not to tell anyone of this."

Alberta pretended to zip her lip. "Not a word."

"I wish he had been here do the baptism last Sunday. That Jarrod was useless in the baptistery. He almost drowned Barbara Ann," said Aggie.

Alberta cast her mind back, remembering Barbara Ann's baptism. She suppressed a smile with an effort.

"Are you sure you don't want to wait for Pastor Teddy, Barbara Ann?"

"I've thought about it, and I don't need to have Pastor Teddy baptize me. Besides, Pastor Jarrod has been so nice to me since I agreed to be one of the flying angels, I think I would like for him to baptize me. The sooner I'm baptized, the sooner I'm a child of God."

Alberta nodded. "I see what you're saying," said Alberta. She folded the white robe and put it into a bag. "It was nice of you to wash this for us. Perhaps that can be your ministry from now on, keeping the robes washed."

"Oh, Miss Alberta, could I?"

"Of course you can, now hurry and get changed. The service is about to start." She opened the door and shooed Barbara Ann in the direction of the changing room. She went into the sanctuary to await the service.

I hope everything goes well for Barbara Ann's sake, she thought. Dear knows what Pastor Jarrod will do. She leafed through the hymn book to find the first hymn. Presently Sam walked to the pulpit and announced the first hymn. "We'll open by singing 'Onward Christian Soldiers.'" He raised his arms to ready the choir. An enthusiastic but inaccurate rendition of the hymn was soon in full swing.

"Now we'll sing one on Pastor Teddy's behalf. I know we all want him to come home soon." He raised his arms again to start the singing and the choir straggled into 'God Will Take Care of You,'" and wavered to an end.

"I thought we might like to learn a new hymn today. It's very simple and easy to remember. It's called a praise chorus and this is what it sounds like." He raised his arms. "Breathe with me, choir," he whispered loudly. For once the choir came in on time: "With all my heart ..." The choir sang it through twice.

Sam turned toward the congregation. "Everyone

try it now."

"Humph!" muttered Aggie under her breath. "If he expects to fly those kiddy songs here, Teddy won't be happy. Waste of time, just a pure waste of time. I'll have a word with him when he comes home." She clamped her lips shut and refused to let even one note escape her.

"God is indeed good," said Sam. "Today He will receive one of our own into His fellowship."

The lights rose in the baptistry. Presently Jarrod splashed into view. He lost his balance and grabbed wildly for the hand rail to no avail. The waters of the baptistry sloshed up to the edge of the tank and spilled over onto the choir seated on the highest risers. A suppressed giggle ran through the congregation.

"Couldn't he have heated that a little?" one of the basses muttered.

Jarrod struggled to his feet, and wiped the water out of his eyes, then reached out for Barbara Ann's hand. The baptistery water rose dangerously close to the point of overflowing again. Barbara Ann shivered as the cold water seeped into the material of her robe and touched on her warm skin.

Jarrod began the liturgy. "Barbara Ann has made her decision and to the fulfillment of that decision," he turned his attention to Barbara Ann, "I baptize you my sister ..." He placed the handkerchief over Barbara Ann's mouth and nose, then tipped her backwards into the water. Her feet rose to the surface. She gasped for air and grabbed for the edge of the tank sending another shower onto the basses. Jarrod seized her arm and helped her into an upright position. Barbara Ann struggled out of the baptistry as the congregation clapped their approval and welcome. Jarrod tried to follow her out, but then he fell, as the water had filled his waders to the brim. He sat down with a thump on the top step and pulled off the waders as best he could. Soon he rose and squelched his way out of sight.

Alberta's attention came back to the present. "I'm sorry, Aggie, my mind wandered and I didn't catch what you said."

"I just said that I wished that Jarrod could clean up his act. He won't find a pulpit botching things."

Chapter 8

"Pageant's only a week away," said Alberta. She made herself more comfortable in the armchair in Lizzie's kitchen. "We'll soon have to put our plan into action." She rifled through the stack of rosters on her lap. "How many people know about it now?"

"Just Grannie Banks and Mrs. Doniphan." Lizzie filled the kettle at the sink. "I swore them to secrecy. Not that they weren't delighted to participate."

Alberta snorted a laugh. "I don't suppose they were hard to convince."

Lizzie plugged the coffee urn in and poured the kettle full of water into it to begin heating. "They thought it was a great idea."

"They didn't even think it was a nasty deal?"

"Grannie Banks said: 'Oh, that's an awful trick,' and giggled. She's been waiting her chance ever since Jarrod was hired. Neither she nor Mrs. Doniphan wanted him here in the first place. He found out about it soon after he came here and said some mean things about them in their hearing. They've been waiting all this time to get even."

"That's around years isn't it?" Alberta looked up from the papers she was shuffling. "They don't hold grudges much, do they?"

Lizzie pulled out a chair and sat down. "They don't actually hold grudges, but they never forget a slight. Besides, Jarrod shouldn't have said anything to begin with."

"I remember that." Alberta arranged her lists on the table. "He was nasty from the start. What surprises me is why someone hasn't called him on a lot of things before now."

The coffee urn began to gurgle. Lizzie rose to check the water level. "From what I've heard, he only does and says things when no one else is around. That way it's his word against whoever he's been harassing."

"Sneaky little rat, isn't he?"

"And of course, no one will say anything against him

because we're taught to respect our 'betters.'" Lizzie shook her head. "Women are brought up to be sweet and compliant, especially in church."

"And especially to men, too. So he's got a double hold on the situation."

"Not anymore, thanks to you," said Lizzie. She settled into a straight chair by the table.

"No, thanks to us," said Alberta. "We can't do it alone. We have to rely on each other."

"That reminds me," said Lizzie. "We don't have to take every single woman out of the congregation, just the ones in key positions."

"You're right," said Alberta. None of the others need to know a thing about it. All we need to do is cull their names from the list, and it'll make the operation that much more efficient and not so likely to be found out."

The doorbell rang. "We can do that this evening when everyone is here." Lizzie rose to answer the door.

"I found Teddy," said Molly. She filtered through front

door of the hot tub store and shed her coat.

"You did?" Lucy kicked off her shoes and stuck her toes into the warm water in the demonstration model. She eased into the water without a ripple. "Where is he?" She slid down into the water as far as her chin. "Mm, lovely. It's so cold out there today."

Molly sat on the edge of the tub and pulled her winter boots off. "You'll never guess."

"Probably not, so you'd better tell me."

"He's at a clinic in Toronto getting dried out." Molly dropped her boot on the floor and swung her feet over the edge of the tub. She stuck her feet into the water up to her shins. "You're right, Lucy, this little side excursion warms my heart."

"So, how'd you find him?" Lucy ran her fingers under the surface of the water creating a slight swell.

"It wasn't easy. Some of those people who are supposed to be helping people aren't." She stretched her toes and flexed her feet. "How d'you turn this thing on?"

"Push the button. I'd have done it for us but I don't

have that much power."

Molly pushed the button and the water began to swirl around their legs and torsos. The salesman looked up from the newspaper he was reading and frowned.

"Hey, Ed, did you put this thing on automatic?"

"No such thing on that model." Ed's voice came from the sales office. "Must not have turned the thing completely off."

The salesman shrugged and went back to his reading. Molly turned over in the pool and availed herself of the warm massage.

"I suppose Teddy was overjoyed to see you." Lucy crossed her legs at the knees and pulled them in to release some of the accumulated tension of the past few weeks.

Molly shook her head. "Uh uh, no. He didn't know I was there."

"You mean, that you didn't manifest to him?"

"Of course, not. It was the one good thing he's done for himself in a long time. Seeing me there would only have spoiled it for him. We want him to recover, not resort to the vitamins again."

"So you had a hard time tracing him." Lucy pulled her legs into a yoga position, and rested her wrists on her knees.

Molly laughed. "You bet I did. I had to upset a few stacks of tickets and file folders to find what I wanted. That poor fellow trying to reconcile the money with the ticket sales just couldn't keep those things on the desk. I heard him say something about needing a vacation in Vancouver."

"Oh, Molly! Shame on you!"

"It was the only way I could see them in sequence. He needed some exercise anyway."

"Oh," said Lucy, "while you were away I heard Alberta talking to Lizzie. They're having another strategy meeting this week. I think it's tonight."

"I guess we should be there." Molly turned off the jets to the hot tub. "We can't afford to have too many things go on without knowing about them."

The salesman looked up at the sudden silence. Molly wafted over to the desk wringing out her towel as she went. The largest of the drops splashed onto his newspaper. "There!" said Molly, "that should give him something to think about."

The meeting was just to the cookie stage when Molly and Lucy settled themselves on top of the refrigerator at Lizzie's house.

"Good, we're not late." Molly pulled her royal purple caftan into place over her knees. She pulled her orange and yellow turban off her head and ran her fingers through her hair. "Mm, that feels better."

"We'd better get down to brass tacks this evening," said Alberta. "With or without Teddy we're committed to this project."

"Has anyone heard from him?" asked Jane.

Alberta shook her head. "Not a peep. I wouldn't even know how to begin to find him." She pursed her lips. "I hope he's alright."

"Would there be some reason that he wouldn't be?" asked Jane.

"He's having a difficult time just now. Between Aggie and Jarrod, he doesn't have much of a life."

"Neither at home nor at work," said Lizzie. She passed the plate of cookies one more time.

"But we're going to fix that for him, aren't we ?" said Barbara Ann. She reached for the last cookie and peered into her coffee cup. "Coffee's kind of low. Not enough here to dunk my cookie." She held out her mug to Lizzie. "Please and thank you."

Lizzie filled Barbara Ann's mug to the top. "That enough?"

"Lots, thank you." She stirred in two spoonfuls of sugar, then overflowed the mug adding milk. She mopped up the spill with her napkin. "We are going to fix it for him, aren't we?"

"If we're successful in our plan, we'll be able to make it so that he can fix it himself," said Maggie.

"And that's better," said Barbara Ann.

Molly and Lucy applauded silently from the top of the refrigerator. "Way to go, Maggie." Molly prodded Lucy gently with her elbow. "We sure picked some winners this time."

"We did, didn't we." Lucy nodded.

"Here are the programs for the pageant, Miss Alberta." Jarrod dumped his sheet on top of the bulletins Alberta was typing. "I want three hundred of them by tomorrow morning."

Alberta picked up the pages for the program from her other work. She scanned the pages and frowned. "Jarrod, why didn't you give me this two weeks ago? I could have had them copied at the copy place. I just don't have time to do this by tomorrow morning."

"You'll do fine, I'm sure, Miss Alberta. Tomorrow morning at nine." He turned and hastened back to his office.

"I'll do fine, Mr. Jarrod, if I stay here until midnight again tonight." She looked over the whole program with more attention. "Good grief, he wants it in colour and glossy too," muttered Alberta.

The office door creaked open. "D'you always talk to yourself?" Jane set her briefcase down on the floor and lowered herself onto the remaining moulded chair.

"Only when conditions are right," said Alberta, "and they are right now!" She handed the pages over to Jane. "Take a gander at these."

"Jarrod's latest contribution to the health and welfare of the Church of the Misbegotten?" They had nicknamed Saint. Bridget's that name when Jarrod had only been there six weeks and had already shown them his true colours. Jane leafed through the pages. "That man needs his own secretary." She handed the pages back to Alberta.

"He needs a keeper, more likely." Alberta stuck her blue pencil behind her left ear.

"We only have another week to go before pageant starts, then you'll get a break."

"Thank goodness," said Alberta.

"Oh, guess who I thought I saw today?"

Alberta shrugged. "I don't know, Santa Claus?"

"No. I think I saw Pastor Teddy."

"Where?" Alberta's smile was wide.

"If I didn't know better, I'd say you were missing him," said Jane. "I saw him, if it was him, down at the main post office. He was posting what looked like post cards."

"Why would he be mailing cards from there? I'd have thought he'd have mailed any post cards he was going to send from wherever he was."

"As I just said, if it was him."

"This is our last rehearsal before the pageant." Jarrod rapped on the desk to gain the cast's attention.

Laurie smiled at Jarrod with just a hint of mischief sparkling in her eyes. "That's right, girls. It's our last rehearsal so listen to Mr. Jarrod. Next time we do it for real."

The cast and crew quieted.

"Good, thank you, Laurie." Jarrod cleared his throat.

"Places everyone." The actors shuffled into their opening places. "Let the play begin."

"Let's do," muttered Laurie. She continued smiling at nothing in particular.

"Laurie, wipe that smile off your face. The opening scene is sombre. We don't need any histrionics at this late date."

Laurie exchanged glances with Sarah and straightened her features into a suitable expression.

"Good evening, Mith Alberta." Teddy eased the office door shut behind himself. "It's late. Why are you still here?"

Alberta looked up from her typing. Her eyes lighted at the sight of Teddy. "You're home, Teddy. Welcome. This place has gone to the dogs in your absence."

"Pastor Jarrod?" Teddy unbuttoned his coat and pulled his scarf away from his neck.

Alberta nodded. "Don't tell anyone you heard it here.

He's been overbearing and demanding the whole time."

"Is that why you're still here?"

"Yes. He left me with all this printing and typing to do before nine tomorrow. He wants it glossy too." Alberta rolled her eyes. "He'll be lucky if I get it together on paper soon enough to make copies."

"I see. Well, Mith Alberta, you just finish the typing. I'll take care of Pastor Jarrod."

"Bless you, Teddy. I'm so tired. It has been rewrite this and copy that ever since you left. I haven't been home at a reasonable time for the past three weeks." Alberta returned to her typing.

Teddy stood looking down at Alberta. He savoured the look of her grey hair and the incipient wrinkles around her eyes. Her bushy grey eyebrows pushed up from behind her glasses. She looks so homey, though Teddy.

Alberta looked up from her task. "Is there something you need, Pastor Teddy?"

"Not really. I guess I forgot what you looked like."

Alberta looked startled. "What difference does it make what I look like?"

"No difference at all." He continued to gaze at Alberta. She cleared her throat and changed the subject. "Have you been home yet?"

"Not yet. I'm not looking forward to it." Teddy frowned. "How has Mummy been?"

"Upset," said Alberta. She has been here every day looking for you. I think she thinks I was aware of your location and that I was covering for you."

"In other words, like a bear with a sore paw."

Alberta chuckled. "You said it, not me." She looked up at Teddy. "You're certainly looking rested. That little vacation must have been what the doctor ordered." He looks healthier, she thought. He's more in touch than I've seen him since high school.

"Thank you, Mith Alberta. It wath exactly what I needed." He straightened his scarf and began buttoning his coat. "I must go home and let Mummy know I'm back." He opened the door and stood for a moment looking back at Alberta. "I'll deal with Jarrod in the morning. Don't stay too late. It's only programs, you know."

Alberta smiled. "It's not as if the story hasn't been told a thousand times."

"Good night, Mith Alberta. I'll thee you in the morning. Tell Jarrod I want to see him first thing."

"I will, Pastor Teddy. Good night. Safe home." She turned back to her typing.

Jarrod slammed Teddy's office door and strode up the hall. His face was bright red, nearly matching his hair. "You little snitch. You told him that you're overworked." He towered over Alberta at her desk. "As far as I can see, all you do all day is drink coffee and gossip with your friends."

Alberta rose from her chair. "As a matter of fact, I didn't volunteer the information, he asked me, and as far as I can see he needs to know what's been happening in his absence." Alberta rose to refill her coffee cup. "As for the coffee, I supply it to this office out of my own pocket, and I'll drink it whenever I want to, thank you very much. Now, if you want those programs for tonight, clear out of here and let me get them finished." She stood with her hands on her hips and looked holes through Jarrod.

Jarrod turned and slammed out of the office. "You're going to be very sorry, Miss Alberta." The door closed behind him with a hiss from the closer.

Alberta dropped her hands from her hips and took a deep breath. "Good riddance," she muttered.

Teddy came up behind her. "Is this how he treats you when I'm not here?"

Alberta startled. "Pastor Teddy. This is the worst it has been. He's been demoted again so I suppose that's stuck in his craw." She moved around the desk and sat down. "If I don't get these finished and copied by noon he'll not have his programs. Thank goodness I have a good relationship with the printer."

"Where are the cast and crew? It's almost time to begin."

Jarrod stomped back and forth outside the dressing rooms. His red hair looked like the burning bush of the Bible, his freckled face looked about to explode. "Steve!" He grabbed one of the shepherds by the arm. "Where is everyone?"

Steve shrugged. "I don't know. I heard that Laurie and the other girls were going to have supper and then come here. That's all I know." He pulled his arm out of Jarrod's grasp. "I have to get my makeup on, except I don't see Judy anywhere." He wandered off down the hall.

Jarrod began his restless stomp once more. "Junior! Have you seen any of the girls?"

Junior shook his head. "Not hide nor hair. They'd better step on it. Steve is in there trying to put on his own makeup. It's frightening to watch. He's going to do the others too." He turned toward the makeup room. "See you in the movies."

Jarrod's stomp took him down the hall to Alberta's office. He pushed the door hard against the wall. "At least you're here."

"Good evening, Jarrod. What can I do for you?"

"Call some of those girls and tell them to hustle. It's almost time to start and the sanctuary is starting to fill up."

"I'd do that, except they've all called in sick."

"Where are their understudies?" Jarrod began to pace the small office.

"There are no understudies. Remember, you didn't want them." Alberta suppressed a smile. "You said it would be a waste of your time."

Alberta watched the thoughts expressing themselves on Jarrod's face.

Jarrod stopped pacing and stood looking down at Alberta. "Miss Alberta, you could help me out of this jam, you know." His voice sweetened and he looked at Alberta with kindness in his eyes. "I'd be eternally grateful."

"Help you do what?" Alberta frowned.

"You could play Mary." Jarrod's voice was syrupy.

"You don't even have to learn any lines. You can just read them off the teleprompter."

"Not on your life," said Alberta. "Get one of the boys to do it. You can pad his toga and put a wig on him and he can read the lines from the teleprompter."

"But he'll have hairy arms and legs."

"So shave him."

Jarrod stood looking at Alberta for several moments. Presently Teddy's office door opened and Teddy emerged. "Jarrod, are you harassing Mith Alberta again?"

"No, but I will if things go much more wrong. She's responsible for this mess."

"What mess?" Teddy looked up at Jarrod. "What's the problem?"

"None of the women showed up to do their parts."

Jarrod's pink cheeks turned almost purple and then paled. "You can help me, Pastor Teddy."

"Oh?" Teddy narrowed his eyes at Jarrod. "What can I do?"

Jarrod managed an ingratiating smirk. "You could play the part of the angel alerting the shepherds. All you'll have to do is make your presence known to the shepherds while the choir sings, 'Hark the Herald Angels Sing'."

"Who's going to be singing if none of the women are here?" asked Teddy.

"The men will have to." Jarrod hastened out the door. "You'll do it, won't you, Pastor?"

Teddy shook his head. "I'll do it."

"Meet with Steve backstage and he'll help you with your harness." The door hissed shut behind him.

"What harness?" Teddy sat down on the moulded chair. "What harness? What do you know about all this? What are you up to?"

"I'm not up to anything," said Alberta. "I'm here where I'm supposed to be. You'd better hustle if you're going to get into your gear."

The lights of the sanctuary dimmed and the spotlight

illuminated Jarrod's head and chest giving him even more of the burning bush effect.

"Ladies and gentlemen." Jarrod picked up a hand mike and his voice came into aural focus. "Thank you all for coming. We have a little problem this evening. All the girls who were to act in the play seem to have fallen ill at the same time, so the boys will be playing their parts and reading the scripts." Jarrod looked over the audience in silence for a moment. "If nothing more, the play will be entertaining." He turned toward the exit. "To that end, let the play begin." He strode out of the glare of the spotlight and tripped going down the stairs. A muffled "Drat!" issued from the darkness stage right.

The opening bars of background music to the play began and the curtains opened. The narrator's rough voice recited:

"And there were in the same country, shepherds abiding in the fields keeping watch over their flocks by night ..."

The recitation of the story continued in the hoarse voice of a teenager insecure in its timbre. "And suddenly there was with the angel a heavenly host ..." The male choir took up the Christmas hymn. "Hark, the Herald Angels Sing." From somewhere in the darkness of the rafters echoed a wail of terror. "No, not that!"

Jarrod's voice came down in a loud whisper: "Just hold Steve's hand and swing out when he does. It'll be alright, and don't forget to sing." Jarrod nodded to Steve who held his hand out to Pastor Teddy. Teddy grabbed Steve's hand and the wooden handrail. "No! No!" Teddy's voice rose several octaves in his fear. Jarrod peeled Teddy's fingers from the handrail and gave him a nudge over the edge, Steve followed, still holding Teddy's hand.

Teddy closed his eyes and swung out over the heads of the audience. The choir plodded through the several verses of "Hark, the Herald Angels Sing." Teddy's wail of fear in the soprano range blended with the all male choir. The harness held and Teddy dangled and swung over the heads of the audience. Steve let go of Teddy's hand.

"No! No!" Teddy's next cry of distress was heard over the choir. The congregation and all the cast looked up and gasped. A concerned murmur went through the crowd. Teddy was hanging by a back strap beneath his wings. His bare feet and hairy legs stuck out from below the edge of his billowing gown. His wings hung askew after his first and second swing.

"Oh, I wish I had my vitaminth." His swing in the straps became less and less until he came to a complete stop over the front rows of pews just on the edge of the spotlight. He dangled about ten feet above Aggie's head. Aggie looked up. Her mouth opened as if she wanted to say something, then her eyebrows drew down into a fierce scowl.

"Cover yourself, Teddy!" Her voice deepened in her rage. "I'll see you at home."

"Not if I thee you firtht," Teddy whispered. He tried the buckles on the strap. "At least they're tholid." He swayed gently on the end of the rope. "How do I get down?" he whispered to Steve.

"Swing," said Steve. "Like this." Steve began to pump his arms and legs and his swing increased. "When you get high enough and close enough to the platform, grab it and climb." Steve's flailing arms and legs increased the scope of his swing until he was nearing the edge of the platform. "I'll go first and grab you, Pastor."

Teddy continued to dangle. "Don't you miss!" He scowled at Steve and tried and failed to gather the hem of his robe at the same time.

"Pump, Pastor." Steve grabbed the edge of the platform on the edge of the balcony and scrambled to relative safety. "More, Pastor." His voice was urgent.

Teddy put more effort into his pumping arms and legs. The audience and cast stared at his predicament in open-mouthed silence. Jarrod ran around in front of the stage waving his arms at the cast. "Action! Action!"

"There's already plenty of that." The voice came out of the darkness of the pews. The cast continued to stare. The spotlight beamed a path of brightness toward Teddy and Steve.

"C'mon, Pastor, you can do it." Steve reached out his hand for Teddy and clasped Teddy's wrist at the height of his swing.

Teddy held on with a strength he didn't know he owned. "Pleath, God," he muttered, "I don't destherve thith."

"You deserve it all and more." Aggie opened her walker and stomped her way toward the door. "Just wait 'til I get you home." Her voice rose above the mutter of the audience.

"You'll not see me home, at least not tonight," said Teddy under his breath. He scrabbled to the dubious safety of the elevated platform.

Chapter 9

The office door swished open. Alberta looked up from her typing. "Oh, it's you, Teddy. Are you okay?" She rose from her chair behind the desk.

Teddy nodded. "I'm a little thore in my shoulderth. That strap was not built for comfort."

Alberta helped Teddy off with his coat. "Aggie's been calling here every five minutes since I came in."

Teddy closed his eyes and moaned slightly. "Have you brewed the coffee yet, Mith Alberta?"

"It's fresh ten minutes ago." Alberta hung Teddy's coat on the coat rack and poured him a cup of coffee. "Have you not been home?"

Teddy sat down with a thump on the nearest stacking chair and shook his head. "I didn't have the strength to deal with Mummy last night. I went to a motel."

Alberta handed him his coffee. "I can understand that." She refilled her own cup. "Aggie's on the warpath alright. I don't think I've ever seen her this angry.

Whatever possessed you to leap from the rafters in one of Jarrod's homemade trusses?" She sat down on her chair and frowned across at Teddy.

Teddy moaned again. "If I'd known what he had in mind he'd never have gotten me up there." He blew on his coffee. "He had me in the robe and up the ladder and into the harness so fast I didn't have time to protest, I didn't really catch on until it was almost too late." He sipped from the edge of his cup. "As it was, he finally pushed me."

Alberta regarded him through the steam from her mug. She drew her bushy eyebrows down into a scowl of concern. "He pushed you?"

Teddy nodded and leaned back against the wall. "He had to pry my fingers off the rail to do it, but he definitely pushed me."

"He could have killed you!"

Teddy sighed and closed his eyes. "I know he could have, but he didn't."

A rush of cold air whistled in under the crack in

the office door. The click and thump of Aggie's walker came with it.

Teddy sat up and set down his cup. "That's Mummy. I'm not here today and I never have been and you don't know where I am." He stood, grabbed his coat and hastened down the back hallway.

The office door whooshed open and Aggie struggled through. "You might at least help me, Alberta."

Alberta came around her desk and pulled the door open all the way. "I'm sorry, Aggie, you were a little too fast for me."

Aggie shuffled to the nearest chair and sat down with a thump. "I suppose you still don't know where Teddy is."

Alberta shook her head. "I have no idea."

"I'll bet you don't," said Aggie. She eyed Alberta for signs of a lie.

"No, as a matter of fact, I really don't. Can I get you a cup of coffee?"

"If that's the least you can do." Aggie shrugged out

of her coat. "Whose mug is that?"

"Barbara Ann was just here. You just missed her." Alberta put a rounded teaspoon's worth of sugar into the mug and stirred vigorously then added powdered creamer. She handed the steaming brew to Aggie.

Aggie took a sip and swallowed quickly. "You put sugar in this!" Her voice raised to its scolding tone. "You know I never take sugar."

"I'm so sorry. I'd forgotten," said Alberta. She suppressed a tiny smile.

"I'll bet you did." Aggie set the mug down on the desk with a little crash. The coffee splashed over the edge and onto the correspondence Alberta had been working on. "Excuse me, Alberta, I splashed."

"It doesn't matter, it's on the disc." Alberta mopped at the mess with a wad of tissue. "Is there anything else I can help you with, Aggie?"

"Humph! You haven't been any help yet. I don't know how you can help me with anything more." Aggie picked up her mug again and sipped at it cautiously. Finding it to her temperature, she swallowed the coffee in two long drafts then belched. "Since you're not going to tell me where Teddy is, I'll go look for him myself." She stood and put on her coat again.

Alberta held the door open for Aggie. "It's lovely to see you again, Aggie."

"Not rushing me out or anything, are you?" Aggie navigated her walker through the door.

"I'll hold the outside door for you too."

Alberta felt a draft around her ankles as the back door opened and closed. She looked up to see Teddy heading toward his office with his briefcase under his arm.

"The coast is clear, Teddy." She rose and went to Teddy's door.

"She's gone?" Teddy shifted the weight of his brief case to his other arm. "Thank you, Mith Alberta, I don't know what I'd do without you." His eyes filled with tears.

"Oh, Teddy, I really don't mind, you know."

Teddy blinked back further tears. "Mith Alberta, I'm so tired of dealing with Mummy. It's never ending and she's never happy no matter what I do for her." He sniffed. "I do thank you, Mith Alberta. It gave me a chance to go home and gather up some of my clothes."

"Are you moving out?"

Teddy sighed. "For a little while at least.

"What'll Aggie say about that?" Alberta helped Teddy out of his coat.

"I expect she'll have plenty to say." He kicked out of his overshoes. "But I'm not sure I really care anymore."

"I can understand that." Alberta hung Teddy's coat and scarf on the coat rack in his office.

Teddy looked down at Alberta. "Can you really, Mith Alberta?"

Jane pushed open the office door. "You're still hard at it?" Alberta looked up from her work. "Oh, Jane, come in. Help yourself to coffee. While you're at it, pour me one too, please." She tapped the stack of paper she'd been working with against the desk top to square it. "What time is it?"

"Quitting time." Jane drained the last of the coffee urn into a cup. "You take this. You look like you need it." She handed the mug to Alberta. "So what's been going on?"

"Teddy came in this morning and managed to get out again before Mummy came by." Alberta rested her elbows on her desk and blew across the top of her coffee.

"With a little help from you, no doubt." Jane sat down on the moulded chair and watched Alberta's face.

Alberta nodded. "Between you and me?"

"Of course."

"I think Teddy is getting fed up with Mummy, and is going to break with her soon. He has stayed in a motel ever since the pageant, and I gather from what he says he's been able to avoid Mummy altogether."

"Poor guy." Jane shook her head. "I don't suppose you know where."

Alberta sighed. "He didn't want to tell me but I caught

sight of a motel brochure on his desk and managed to worm it out of him." Alberta sighed again. "I just wish he had the gumption to tell Mummy where to go once and for all. He doesn't deserve to be treated like this."

"Has there been any backlash from the pageant?"

"Lots. There was a picture of Teddy hanging from the rafters and a write-up that surely curled Mummy's hair."

"I didn't know the press was going to be there."

"I didn't either." Alberta shrugged. "But you know Jarrod, anything for publicity."

"How's he been?"

"He's been a bear with a sore paw ever since. Nothing pleases him and he blames it all on me." Alberta rubbed her face hard and sniffed.

"Are you crying?" Jane shoved the box of tissues across the desk. "It's not worth it, you know."

Alberta mopped her eyes and blew her nose. "I know. I just keep coming around to the fact that Teddy doesn't deserve either Mummy or Jarrod."

Jane reached across the desk and patted Alberta's

hand. "C'mon, Alberta. Close up shop and we'll go get a bite to eat. My treat."

"Where are all the Sunday school girls?" Jarrod slammed the stack of choir folders he was carrying onto the top of Alberta's desk. "I had a rehearsal scheduled and none of them showed up." He leaned on his knuckles and stared Alberta in the eyes. "If I didn't think you wanted the best for this church, I'd say you were behind it, Miss Alberta." He bent closer to Alberta and forced her to bend her head back in order to see him.

Alberta rose from her chair. "How dare you treat me like the hired help." She stared back at Jarrod. "I don't know where the girls are, they're not my responsibility, and I don't much care whether you believe me. Now take your folders off my desk, and don't ever speak to me in this fashion again."

Jarrod's face went white and then purple. He grabbed up the folders and backed away from Alberta's desk and sidled out to his office.

Alberta sat down in her chair and rested her head on her bent arms. She wept quietly, the tears absorbed into the desk mat in front of her. She was so absorbed in her misery she did not hear Teddy's door opening and closing.

Alberta sniffed hard and raised her head. "Oh, Teddy, it's Jarrod. I just told him to take a long walk off a short pier. He's spitting mad just now and he's probably in there making a voodoo doll that resembles me." She searched her surroundings for the tissue box. Teddy handed her his clean handkerchief. She mopped her face and wiped her nose. "And I don't care if he is, he's had it coming for a long, long while." She sniffed again.

Teddy sat down on the moulded chair and patted Alberta's arm. "I know he deserved it and I'm glad you stood up to him." Teddy's eyes were soft with sympathy. "And I also know that there's something going on around here that all the ladies know about and the men don't, and you're in on it."

Alberta leaned her head back and and stared at the

ceiling. "There is, but I can't tell you about it." She closed her eyes and sniffed again. "I just didn't think I'd ever be in the middle."

Teddy continued to pat Alberta's arm. "I'll not press you for an explanation, and if it smartens thingth up around here it will be to the good."

"Bless you, Teddy. I wish I could keep you from being in harm's way, but I can't."

"Where are all the sopranos and altos this evening?" Sam surveyed the empty rows on the choir risers. "Is your wife sick, Dave?"

Dave shrugged his shoulders. "I don't know. She left home a little before me. I assumed she was coming here as usual."

"I hope nothing's happened to her." Sam stood in contemplation for a moment. "I guess we'll rehearse your parts for Sunday."

"Why don't you make us a double quartet. There are eight of us here so it should work out right."

Sam nodded. "Good thinking, Ray. We'll do a warm up first. It'll have to be a capella since our pianist is not here either."

Maggie Morley pushed through the office door. "Are you up for lunch yet?" She sat down and opened her coat. "I heard there's a good eats place just opened downtown."

Alberta stretched her shoulders back and rolled her head around to loosen the knots that typing always put in her neck. "Any time. I can't wait to get away from here today." She rose to get her coat. "This stuff can wait."

"What's up? You look worn to a frazzle."

"Whatever you say." Maggie buttoned her coat again. "I hardly need this today. We're in the middle of the January thaw."

Alberta grunted a laugh. "Spring can't come soon enough." She shrugged into her own coat. "I'll just tell Teddy I'm going."

Presently they seated themselves at the newest restaurant in town.

"It's certainly shiny enough in here," said Alberta.
"Even the floors are reflective." She looked around.
"They look as if they could have supported the whole
plastics industry by themselves."

"I wonder how long it will last?" Maggie shrugged
out of her coat and picked up the shiny new menu.
"Let's see what they're offering."

"Food, I hope," said Alberta. She looked over her
own menu.

"Are you ready to order, ladies?" The waitress
appeared out of nowhere. She pulled a bright red pencil
from behind her ear and poised it over the pad.

Alberta and Maggie made their choices and the waitress disappeared into the recesses of the kitchen.

Maggie leaned toward Alberta and spoke softly. "Did
you get a load of that plastic tiara?"

Alberta chuckled. "I had a hard time keeping a straight
face." She leaned back in her seat and sighed. "That's
the first laugh I've had since before Thanksgiving."

"So how're things going?"

Alberta ran her fingers through her hair and sighed again. "Terrible. Between Mummy and Jarrod it hasn't been much fun."

"I suppose not, and you have to field all the questions from Mummy and all the crap from Jarrod." Maggie sat back, startled by her own use of the word 'crap.'

"And that's just what it is," said Alberta. "I've been trying to find a word for it myself."

"How much longer do you think it will take?"

"Not much, I hope. I don't know how much more I can stand." She rubbed her face with her hands. "I understand that Teddy has to steer clear of Mummy just now 'til he knows for sure what he's going to do, but Jarrod has no excuse."

"Perhaps we need another meeting."

"It will be good to have a few cookies, if nothing else, and I can surely use the support."

Alberta spoke to the ladies who had assembled in Lizzie's kitchen. "I truly didn't know that this would go on as long as it has. I thought we'd have made our point by the end of the Christmas pageant. It is becoming a burden to me and I'm not sure how much longer I can keep it up."

"Lent is almost upon us, and Jarrod'll be wanting another extravaganza for Easter," said Jane.

"I know," said Maggie, "he never quits."

"I don't think we should give up now," said Sandra. "We've come too far to just let it go."

"I can't understand why the men in the congregation haven't caught on yet," said Lizzie.

"Maybe they know and are secretly cheering us on," said Barbara Ann.

"That may be true," said Sandra. "I heard my John talking to Jeff next door the other day. I was cleaning windows and had the one in the kitchen open and they were right underneath it. They were saying that they hoped that our siege worked. They said a lot of other things about Jarrod, and about Mummy and Teddy, too."

"My George never liked Jarrod since the day he came," said Lizzie. "The day George died he said to be sure and get Teddy to do the funeral service. He said that at least Teddy knows his way around the preachers' guide and Jarrod just thinks he does."

"John caught him giving the pianist a scolding several years ago. The poor girl was almost in tears. John said he walked up on the platform and cleared his throat which startled Jarrod and he stopped. John has not had much use for him since then."

The group was silent for a few minutes. "D'you think you can stand it for a few more weeks, Alberta?" asked Jane. "The way I'm seeing it just now is that we have to hold his feet to the flame a little longer, otherwise it will have been a waste of our time and we'd have done all this for nothing."

Alberta thought for a moment, then shook her head. "You're right, Jane. I'll just grit my teeth and shoulder on through. I can even try to be pleasant with him."

"We need a real absentee effort, I think," said Lizzie.

"D'you suppose we can get enough of the other women to make a difference by staying away?"

"Convince them not even to offer their services for the Easter Pageant?" asked Jane.

"We'll just need to motivate a core group of women and teenagers. Sally's Laurie is a good little conspirator and can certainly hold her own in any discourse with Jarrod." Maggie drained her teacup. "We're lucky that the women fall into such well defined groups."

"I think that's the way with most organizations," said Alberta. "There are those who do a lot all the time, and there are those who don't want to be involved except to come on Sunday morning."

"So d'you think you can stand a few more weeks of the siege, Alberta?" asked Jane.

"I guess so. If it weren't for the good of the church, and I certainly see your point, I wouldn't. We've only come half way yet, and now is not the time to quit."

"Good for you, Alberta." Molly and Lucy clapped silently

from their perch on top of the refrigeration.

"Go for it," said Lucy, and promptly lost her balance.

Molly grabbed Lucy by the waist band of her skirt and saved her from a fall. "Take it easy," said Molly. "You won't be much use to this enterprise if you break your neck."

Lucy straightened her twin set more neatly around her waist. "I know what we should do."

"What's that?" Molly eyed the last cookie on the plate.

"We should do something nice for Alberta. She has a lot to bear just now."

Molly pursed her lips. "That'd be nice. What d'you have in mind?"

"Oh, a flower on her desk, a new set of pens, the kind that have the nibs like the old fashioned inkwell pens. There's a magazine that she really likes, that she doesn't subscribe to because it's too expensive. She always goes to the library to read it. Little things like that."

'How do you know so much about her likes and dislikes?" asked Molly.

Lucy shrugged. "I like to know who I'm dealing with so I do some research and observation. We really haven't a lot to do besides supervise on this case so I took the opportunity to watch Alberta. I also watched Jarrod and Pastor Teddy."

"You have been busy." Molly looked at the last cookie on the plate just as Jane reached for it. "I'll have that, thank you very much." She grabbed up the cookie from under Jane's hand.

"What happened to that cookie?" asked Jane. She stared at the plate and then at her hand. "I was just reaching for it and it disappeared."

"You probably just thought it was there," said Maggie.

"I'm not given to imagination," said Jane. "It was there a moment ago and I didn't take it." She picked up the plate and looked underneath it.

"Maybe someone else took it," said Lizzie. "Perhaps you had a little time lapse that you didn't notice. That happens sometimes. Can I get you something else? It's no trouble, you know."

Jane continued to stare at the plate and shook her head. "No. No, thank you, Lizzie. I didn't need the cookie anyway."

Chapter 10

"Mith Alberta, d'you have time to do thome typing for me?" asked Teddy.

"Of course." Alberta looked up from her task of sorting through the submissions for the Sunday bulletin. "It's what I'm here for."

She took the sheaf of papers from Teddy and scanned the first page. "It's your sermon for Sunday. You have never asked me to type this before."

Teddy cleared his throat. "I couldn't. Mummy insisted on doing the proofreading. She was a bear about it, so to keep the peace, I just gave in to her."

"This is better than your usual sermon." Alberta looked up at Teddy. "I can't remember when you've given such an inspired talk."

Teddy's face reddened a little. "That wath Mummy's doing. Not to speak ill of her help, but she added and deleted whole sections of the thermon. I never knew what to expect when I went into the pulpit on

Sunday morning."

Alberta frowned. "D'you mean that you hadn't even read it over before you preached?"

Teddy sighed and shook his head. "I couldn't. She never gave it back to me in time. I was always winging it."

"Couldn't you have given a copy to me?" Alberta's eyes scanned the second page. "Or changed it back to the way you had it as you preached?"

Teddy sat down on one of the stacking chairs. "I did that a few times, but there was hell to pay when I got home."

"Aggie must be a worse tyrant than any of us ever guessed. I'm sorry Teddy. Your life has been difficult."

"I could never stand up to Mummy." Teddy sniffed and rubbed his face with his handkerchief. "Mainly because she could always yell louder than I could. I hate being yelled at. It makes me feel so helpless."

"Worthless too, I would guess." Alberta continued scanning the pages of notes.

Teddy nodded. "That too." He rose to help himself to coffee and a tea biscuit. "This'll make me feel better."

The back door by Teddy's office opened and Aggie began her torturous walk down the hallway.

"There you are, Teddy." She pushed forward as fast as her arthritic feet would allow.

Teddy turned, his cookie fell into his coffee and splashed the hot coffee onto his hand. "Mummy!" He made a move to go out the other door.

"Don't bother running away, I know where you're staying." Aggie's breath came in short gasps as she hastened up the hallway. "How dare you avoid me? I've done everything I knew how to improve your life and this is the thanks I get? A son who won't see me, who casts all my help back at me in rudeness and disrespect. I thought I taught you to honour thy father and mother." She stopped in front of Teddy and caught her breath.

Alberta set down the sermon notes. "I have heard that often under the worst circumstances in a person's life."

Aggie turned her attack toward Alberta. "And you! Hiding his whereabouts and covering his tracks for him." She paused for breath again.

"I've had that commandment thrown at me all my life," said Teddy. "Whatever happened to 'parents, provoke not your children?'"

Aggie ignored him and continued her attack on Alberta. "You slut! He's been staying with you, hasn't he. You've got nothing better to do with your life than harbour a wayward son."

Teddy's face went white and then red. "How dare you speak to Mith Alberta like that. She is so far from being a slut that the word doesn't even apply. Now, you apologize to her."

"I'll do no such thing!" Aggie's rage was out of control. "You're living with her and you don't want to admit it."

Teddy grabbed his mother by her arms and shook her. "I'm not living with her. She ith a respectable woman and I would not thay or do anything to tarnish her good name."

"She's trash too." Aggie's face broke into a sweat. "Always hanging around saying, 'Yes, Pastor Teddy, that's right, Pastor Teddy.'"

Teddy turned to Alberta. "Is this what you've put up with all thith time?"

"Something like it, though she's worse now than I've ever seen her."

"You're a fool, Teddy. No better than your father." Aggie's breath was coming in gasps. "She's a splut and you're a fuffle." Aggie's breathing was irregular as she slowly rolled down onto the floor. Her face lost its redness and became pale. "Oh, dear, dear, dear." Her spittle foamed against her lips and she thrust her tongue in and out.

"Mummy!" Teddy knelt down beside her and patted her face. "Mummy!"

"Dear, dear, dear, dear." Aggie continued to work her tongue against her teeth. Her saliva ran down her face and was soaked up by the carpet."Dear, dear, dear."

She looked up at Teddy. "Oh, dear, dear, dear."

Teddy looked up at Alberta. "Call an ambulance, Mith Alberta."

"I already have. They're on their way." She handed a wad of tissue to Teddy. "Wipe off her face."

The ambulance came and went and Teddy followed. Alberta picked up Teddy's sermon notes and scanned them. They are better than usual. She read them more closely.

Pastor Teddy you're got the spirit of a fine preacher. Who would've guessed? She settled into her chair and began typing. The notes were still coffee stained and Teddy's handwriting still had the annoying wiggle in it that had been there since his youth, but the concepts he was presenting shone out from the pages as never before.

Alberta startled as someone spoke her name. Her hand went to her chest. She turned and blinked at Jane. "Oh, it's you. I didn't hear you come in."

Jane shed her coat and seated herself in the moulded

chair. "I know. I spoke to you twice before you heard me. What has you so engrossed?"

"Teddy's sermon. He gave me the unadulterated copy this morning." She handed the first two pages to Jane. "Just read that. It positively shines."

Jane speed read the pages. "I see what you're talking about. How'd you get a copy like this?"

"He brought it to me this morning. Aggie didn't have a hand in it at all."

"How'd he get it past her?" Jane lay the rumpled draft on Alberta's desk. "Didn't you tell me that he wasn't living at home?"

"He's not, so she didn't even get a glance at it. Mummy arrived while he was here and went into an awful tirade about me and Teddy and how he was staying with me and wasn't I just the worst slut. Teddy lost his cool and told her that she couldn't say things like that about me. He was quite magnificent."

"I bet old Aggie was spitting." Jane picked up the pages and began scanning them again.

"Spitting is right," said Alberta. "She took a stroke on the spot and drooled and spit all over herself and the floor."

Jane looked up from her reading. "You're kidding."

"Oh, no. I called the ambulance and Teddy kept mopping her chin. She's gone now to the local hospital. She was quite incapacitated and could only say 'dear, dear, dear.'"

"That'll slow her down. She always has to have the last word." Jane read the last page again. "Not that I wish her any harm."

"Neither do I, but what goes around, inevitably comes around one way or another." Alberta clasped her hands behind her head and stretched her shoulders. "I'm about done here. I was kind of making work until I heard from Teddy." She squared the edges of the sermon on the edge of the desk. "I'll just put these on Teddy's desk. Why don't you come home and have a bite to eat with me."

Jane settled herself on the tall stool beside the bar that served as a table in Alberta's small kitchen. "I have some news." She watched Alberta peeling vegetables.

"Oh?" Alberta's hands stilled on the carrot she was peeling. "I'm all ears."

"I had a call from Sam last evening. He's taking me out to dinner and a show tomorrow."

Alberta turned to look at Jane. "What prompted this?"

"I'm not sure." Jane frowned. "I hope he's not going to pump me for information."

Alberta shook her head. "He's not devious like that. In any case, he asked me for your telephone number before Christmas pageant."

"And you never told me?"

Alberta shook her head. "No, I figured it was your collective business and if anything came of it I'd hear about it."

"You are a clam, aren't you?"

"I've learned over the years." The telephone rang and she picked up the receiver. "Hello?" She waited for the party to reply. "Teddy. How's your mother?" She listened for his reply. "I'm just making supper for Jane and me. Why don't you come by? It won't be any hardship to put another potato in the pot. See you in a while then." She hung up the receiver and turned to Jane. "They've taken Aggie by ambulance to the hospital in Charlottetown. They have a stroke unit there. She's not doing well."

"That's too bad." Jane was silent for a moment. "How old is she?"

Alberta returned to peeling vegetables. "She's approaching eighty, I think. Teddy was born the same year I was, and she wasn't young then."

Teddy stepped into the office and closed the door gently behind himself. "Thank you for a fine supper last evening, Miss Alberta. I've enjoyed this more than any meal I've had in a long time." His face flushed.

Alberta turned away from her typing. "You're more than welcome, Teddy. How's your mother doing?"

Teddy perched on the edge of the moulded chair. "Not well, Mith Alberta. Not well at all."

"Would you like a cup of coffee? I miscounted the number of spoons of grounds, so it's extra fortifying today."

Teddy nodded and leaned back in the chair. "That's just what I need."

"Have you seen Aggie since yesterday?" Alberta set a mug of coffee beside Teddy.

"Thankth, Miss Alberta, you're a gem." Teddy sipped from his mug. "I was down to the hospital this morning. They're not very hopeful for much rehabilitation. It was quite a severe stroke. She actually ruptured an aneurysm. She's flaccid on one side and can't thay any thing except 'dear, dear, dear.'" Teddy sipped again.

"It must be hard for you to see her like that. She's always been so feisty." Alberta filled up her mug again, then sat down at the desk.

"She's in a thort of intensive care unit for strokes. I'm only allowed in ten minuteth at a time, but she got tho upset when I was there the nurses told me that it might be better if I sthayed away for a day or two." Teddy sighed and closed his eyes.

"Have you had any sleep since last night?" Alberta leaned on her elbows and regarded Teddy over the rim of her mug.

Teddy shook his head. "I went back to the house after your wonderful thupper and dozed on the couch until midnight then I went to bed and lay there and watched car lights going across the ceiling and when traffic became less frequent I started playing number gameth with the digital clock. I wath quite good with mental arithmetic when I was young." Teddy sighed again. "When I wath young."

"Now Pastor Teddy, you're not that old yet."

Teddy sighed. "I feel as if I'm about twice my age thometimes."

"Jane and I were figuring out Aggie's age the other day, and I remembered that you and I are the same age almost to the day." Alberta picked up several pencils and ran them through the sharpener. "Besides, you don't even look fifty yet despite all your trials." She returned her pencils to the pencil mug and sat regarding Teddy's round pink face with a serious expression."

Teddy reached across the desk and patted Alberta's forearm. "Thank you for thaying that, Mith Alberta." He rose to leave. "You truly are a gem."

Alberta sat in stunned silence and watched Teddy down the hall to his office. That's the nicest thing he's ever said to me, she thought. What a waste of a good man.

"Close your mouth, Miss Alberta, he's a Mummy's boy, and always will be." Jarrod dropped a handful of papers on Alberta's desk. "Thirty copies collated by this evening."

Alberta turned and looked up at Jarrod's freckled face. "By this evening?"

"By this evening." Jarrod leered down at her. Think you can do it without too many thoughts about lover boy?"

Alberta stood up and picked up the pages and handed them back to Jarrod. "Do it yourself." She turned and walked out of the office and hastened to the women's room. It's like I'm scared of Jarrod or something, she chided herself, taking refuge in the ladies. I wonder if he'll do his own copying. I guess I'll know soon enough.

Alberta dawdled in the wash room as long as she could stand it. She washed her hands and mopped up the basin with some paper towel. She sat on the chaise longue and leafed through an abandoned church magazine. She inspected her nails. I must tidy them up one of these days, she thought. She washed her hands again and ran her comb through her hair. I'll try and slip out by Teddy's door, she thought. She stuck her head out the door of the ladies' room and saw that the coast was clear. I feel like a criminal, she thought. Jarrod sure has a way of tarnishing perceptions. She opened the door to her office quietly, snatched her purse from under the desk, shut down the computer and hastened out the back door.

"Where'd you get to tho fast yesterday?" asked Teddy.

"She was running away from me," said Jarrod. "I asked her to do some copying and collating for me and she refused. I think she was actually trying to hide out in the ladies' from me, but I just postponed the job." He slammed the sheaf of papers onto Alberta's desk and turned to leave. "As I asked you yesterday, thirty copies collated by noon."

"Wait a minute!" said Teddy. "Is that how you speak to Mith Alberta? No please, nor thank you?" Teddy placed himself in Jarrod's path and stood staring up at Jarrod's freckled face. "Is this how he treats you, Mith Alberta?"

Alberta rose from her seat behind her desk and stepped as far back into the corner as she could. "Usually. Sometimes worse."

"Apologize to Mith Alberta immediately." Teddy stood with his hands on his hips like a bantam rooster.

Jarrod shrugged. "I apologize, Mith Alberta." He towered over Teddy and smiled down at him. He stepped aside to pass Teddy and disappeared into his office.

Teddy's face lost some of its ruddiness. "Oh," he said, "that man ith living on borrowed time." He turned to Alberta. "What did he thay yesterday?"

Alberta sat down behind her desk and stared at the desk blotter. "It's not worth repeating, Pastor Teddy. He was being rude and crude as he always is."

"Always?"

"Ever since he started here." Alberta shifted in her chair.

"He must have had you quite upset for you to take refuge in the ladies.' He sat down across the desk from Alberta. "Can't you tell me?"

"He made some crude remarks about you and me, and that's all I'm going to say." She picked up the sheaf of papers and rose from her chair. "I must get this done, the less contact I have with that man the better." She kept her eyes averted as she turned and headed in the direction of the copying closet.

Alberta unlocked her front door that evening and hastened inside and shut it behind herself. If I ever spend another day in that office it'll be the end of me, she thought. She kicked off her snow boots in the vestibule and pattered in stockinged feet into the hallway. She hiccuped. I've got to stop drinking that awful coffee. She rubbed her stomach and hiccuped again. In the kitchen she flopped into the old armchair that had been her grandfather's and closed her eyes. Presently the telephone rang. It was Jane.

"Oh, hello, Jane. I just got in. What's your news?"

"You'll never guess."

"So tell me then." Alberta propped her feet on the ottoman.

Jane drew a big breath and continued. "Sam knows what's going on and has done all the time. Not only that, he approves of it."

"He does?" Alberta sat upright in the old wing chair. "How d'you know that?"

"He told me. He has known almost from the very

beginning. He told me on the QT he was hoping that something like this would happen since he can't do anything about it himself."

"Is that why he took you to dinner?"

"Ah, no."

"Come on Jane, give me the details."

"I'm swearing you to secrecy."

"Cross my heart," said Alberta.

"He wants me to go out with him again. I feel like a silly teenager." Jane's voice held a hint of a giggle.

"D'you want to?"

"Of course, I want to. He's a very nice man and I haven't seen anyone since that unfortunate relationship I had with the English prof."

"In that case, it's about time." Alberta switched the receiver to the other ear. "So where'd he take you?"

"To a tiny Italian restaurant down in Charlotte-town. I didn't even know it was there. Everything was just perfect."

"Sounds nice. You'll have to tell me where he takes

you the next time. Did he kiss you good night?"

"A European peck on the cheek. But that was plenty, and not rude."

"Y'know, you're right. I can't imagine Sam being rude to anyone."

"Well, I mustn't keep you," said Jane. "Keep me posted."

"Mith Alberta, I've typed up a letter regarding Jarrod that's to go to the elders. I'd appreciate it if you can proof it and retype it for me. You're tho much better a typist than I am."

Alberta took the rumpled paper from Teddy. "Hm, I'll do it right away." She scanned the letter. "Who're you sending it to?"

"All of them, I suppose. It wouldn't do to get anyone's nose out of joint on this matter."

"Of course not," said Alberta. "Do you mind if I correct the grammar and spelling?"

"You do whatever needth to be done to it. I'm sure

it can only be improved." Teddy turned and headed toward his office. Alberta watched him go.

He must be off the 'vitamins,' she thought. He has been much more coherent than he used to be, and I think he's losing some weight. Alberta gave a mental shrug. Whatever it is, he's looking better than he has in years. She turned to her computer.

The telephone rang, dragging Alberta out of a dream about flying with an old lady in a purple caftan and an outrageous orange turban. She fumbled for the receiver. "Hello?"

"I'm sorry to waken you so early, Mith Alberta. Mummy hath taken a turn for the worse and my car won't start ... "

Alberta came fully awake. "I'll be right there." She swung her feet over the side of the bed and fumbled for her slippers. In fifteen minutes she was giving an abbreviated toot outside Teddy's house. The ride to town was fast and silent.

She dropped Teddy off at the front door and went in search of a parking place. In a few minutes she was riding the elevator to the third floor. Teddy was in the waiting room sitting with his head in his hands. He looked up to see who had entered. "Mith Alberta! You didn't need to stay."

"It's not good to be alone at times like these." She settled herself on the lumpy couch and began to leaf through some out of date magazines on the side table. "Besides, it's too early to go in to work. The sun isn't even up yet."

Presently a nurse entered. "Are you Aggie's next of kin?"

Teddy jumped to his feet. "I'm her thon."

"I just want to tell you that she has stabilized for now and is asleep. I'll come and get you the moment she wakens."

"Thank you," said Teddy. He sat down again. "This is going to be a long day, Mith Alberta. Are you sure you want to spend it waiting here?"

"It's a good as any. Besides, you really need someone with you right now. This way, I can avoid Jarrod too.

Three hours went by. Teddy paced the waiting room some of the time and sat with his head in his hands at others. Alberta read yesterday's newspaper and watched Teddy out of the corner of her eye. Eventually a nurse came and talked to Teddy.

"She's awake now, and for once she's not particularly agitated. I'll just show you to her room."

Teddy looked at Alberta. "Will you come too, Mith Alberta? It's thilly, I know, but I really don't want to thee her in this state. I just need a little moral thupport."

Alberta rose from the couch and turned to the nurse. "If you think it'll be alright."

"She needs all her family now," said the nurse. Alberta raised a bushy grey eyebrow at Teddy. "What d'you think, Teddy?"

"I can't thee that there would be any harm in coming too. It might lift her opinion of you. It may make her feel better to know that you're waiting with me."

They followed the nurse down the corridor to the unit. She turned in at the first cubicle.

"Miss Aggie, your son and his wife are here." She patted Aggie's face to rouse her from the light sleep she had slipped into.

"Don't go to thleep for a moment, Mummy. Look who I've brought to visit with you."

Aggie turned her head and focused on Alberta. Her eyes widened and her face flushed. "Oh, dear, dear, dear." She began gesticulating and pointing at Alberta with her unaffected hand. "Oh, dear, dear, dear. Oh, dear, dear, dear."

"Now Mummy, I thought you'd be pleathed to see someone from the church, and Mith Alberta was kind enough to drive me all the way here before the crack of dawn."

"Oh, dear, dear, dear." Aggie's agitation was becoming more apparent. Presently the nurse hastened into the cubicle.

"What have you said to her? Her blood pressure just went sky high."

"Oh, dear, dear, dear." Aggie licked her dry lips and began working her tongue against her teeth. "Oh, dear, dear, dear." The heart monitor started beeping and showing an erratic heart rhythm then suddenly no pattern at all.

"Code Blue, Code Blue!" The nurse grabbed the cart and pulled it into the room.

"What'th happening?" asked Teddy. The room became full with many people in white coats. No one answered him.

Alberta grabbed his arm and pulled him out of the cubicle. "Come and sit with me in the waiting room, Pastor Teddy. They have their work ahead of them just now and they don't need us here getting in the way." She steered Teddy back in the direction of the waiting room. "They'll come and let us know when they finish."

Teddy collapsed into an armchair and sat with his head in his hands. "You know, Mith Alberta, as difficult ath she hath been, I don't wish her any harm."

"Of course, you don't, Pastor Teddy. If I know this, the others will know it too." She reached across the arm of the couch and patted Teddy's arm. "You've been a patient and forbearing son to her, and no one can fault you for what happened to Aggie. She brought it on herself."

Chapter 11

Teddy paced the small waiting room. His face was pale and tired looking.

"Shall I go to the cafeteria and get us some coffee?"

"Thank you, Mith Alberta, that's awfully kind of you." Teddy continued to pace. "If I'm not here I'll be in with Mummy."

Alberta picked up her purse and left for the cafeteria. In a few minutes she was back with breakfast for both of them. Teddy was still pacing.

"Pastor Teddy, come and sit down and we'll have our breakfast. There's no telling what you'll have to face today, and you'll be glad for the nourishment." Alberta spread napkins on the coffee table to make place mats and then arranged the pot of coffee in the middle and the plates of toast at each place.

They breakfasted in silence. Presently Alberta set her cup down and said: "Pastor Teddy, why don't you stretch out on the couch and have a nap. You'll feel better for it."

"You're tho kind, Mith Alberta. I think I will." He lay down on his side and punched a couple of ancient throw cushions into a more comfortable shape. In a few minutes he was gently snoring his arm dangling off the edge of the couch. Alberta sat in the armchair and studied his sleep softened face.

He used to be quite cute, she thought. He still has his gorgeous eyelashes. His chubby cheeks have sagged over the years, though I suppose we've all sagged a little here and there. At least his eyebrows haven't gotten hairy. She suppressed a snort of ironic laughter. Unlike my own. She leaned her head against the high back of the chair and drifted off herself.

It seemed no time at all until the nurse was patting her hand to awaken her. Alberta sat up and blinked.

"Ma'am, I'm sorry but she didn't make it." The nurse sat down in the other chair. "Is there anything I can do for you?"

Alberta sighed. "I don't think so. Poor Pastor Teddy.

He was his mother's only son and paid dearly for it." She was silent for a moment watching Teddy's relaxed face and gentle breathing. "I wonder how he'll handle it." She rose and shook Teddy's shoulder. "Pastor Teddy, wake up."

Teddy stirred and blinked. "Yeth, Mith Alberta?"

"I'm sorry to have to tell you, Aggie didn't make it."

Teddy closed his eyes and shook his head. "She made herself a difficult life." He opened his eyes and looked at the nurse. "Have you made any arrangements yet?"

"Not yet. Do you wish to view the remains?"

Teddy shrugged. "I don't know. Let me think about it for a moment." He stared down at his hands turning them over and over again. Presently he stood up. "I will see her now."

"D'you want me to come with you?"

"I think I need to do thith alone, Mith Alberta." Teddy followed the nurse and Alberta sat down to wait for his return. *I wonder who he'll get to preach the funeral sermon?* Her thoughts wandered on. *I wonder* how he'll manage now that she's gone?

Teddy stood at the foot of Aggie's bed looking at his mother. Mummy, you've never looked so good. You know I've always tried to be a good son to you. I feel as if I've failed.

"You haven't failed."

The voice seemed to come from the head of the bed. Teddy looked up to see Molly perched on the head rail of Aggie's bed.

Teddy gasped. "I thought you were only a part of my addiction to vitamins."

"No such luck," said Molly. "I'm as real as you are." She smiled broadly at Teddy.

Teddy looked back at Aggie's slack features. "I wonder where she ith now."

Molly straightened her bright orange turban. "She's over here now. Lucy is taking her to the Sunrise Rest Home. She'll sleep for three weeks to recover from her work on earth, then she'll be wakened to attend school and learn why her life was so miserable."

"She made it that way herself," said Teddy then clamped his lips shut.

"It never pays to speak ill of the dead," said Molly. "Now, go and make the funeral arrangements before she gets any colder."

Teddy stood for a moment longer gazing at his mother's slack features. "Poor Mummy." He shook his head and blinked back tears. I don't know why I have any tears for you, he thought. You made life so miserable for yourself and everyone around you. He turned away.

"I think I'd like to have Walker's Funeral Home take care of the detailth for me." He stopped at the desk. "Is there anything I have to thign?"

"Your mother's valuables are here in our safe. I'll get them for you." The nurse rose from her chair. "Do you want an autopsy?"

A look of horror crossed Teddy's cherubic face. "Heaventh no. Why would I want them to cut up poor

Mummy? It's not as if we don't know why she died."

"Some people like to know for certain. Did she have any thoughts on organ donation?"

Teddy blinked. "Organ donation? I doubt she ever even thought about such a thing." He stood contemplating the idea while the nurse went to fetch Aggie's valuables. Presently the nurse returned.

"You'll have to sign for these." She handed the paper container to Teddy.

"About the organ donation." Teddy bent to sign for the trinkets the nurse called valuable. "I think it's an excellent idea." He handed the pen back to the nurse. "Her death should count for something."

The nurse handed him a sheaf of papers. "Look these over and if you're satisfied with the arrangements sign them on the last page. You are her sole survivor?"

"Thole thurvivor? Yeth, I think that's tho. I am her thurvivor." Teddy smiled a tiny smile of satisfaction.

"Are you ready to leave now?" Alberta gathered up her purse and gloves, then took her coat down from the rack.

"Let me help you with that, Mith Alberta." Teddy took the coat from Alberta's hands.

Alberta's eyebrows rose a tiny half inch. She straightened her expression and turned to allow Teddy to assist her with her coat.

"Who will be taking care of the funeral?"

"Walkerth," replied Teddy. "She hated old man Walker, and didn't much like the thons either."

Retribution? thought Alberta. She pulled her gloves on.

"I've donated her organs to the transplant people." The tiny smile curved onto Teddy's lips.

Alberta's bushy grey eyebrows rose to their maximum height. "She was dead set against organ donation. She said once that she came into the world with all her organs and she'd go out with all her organs, and that was that."

Teddy's smile broadened into a grin. "Yeth, isn't it wonderful? Now she can begin doing good."

"So who's doing the funeral service?" Jane sat down on the moulded plastic chair and unbuttoned her coat.

"Teddy said he was going to do it himself." Alberta turned away from the bulletins she was preparing for the Sunday service.

"Isn't that a little unusual?"

Alberta leaned her elbows on her desk and stroked her lower lip. "It is, but I think he's getting some kind of satisfaction from it. He has been on the phone all morning making arrangements. I think she had some cousins who live in Boston, though I think they're old now too."

"They'll not likely come all the way here just to go to Aggie's funeral, will they?"

"Not likely, if she was as hard on them as she was on poor Teddy."

"So what time is the visitation?"

"Tomorrow evening from 7 'til 8:30 at the funeral home."

Jane slid her arms out of her coat sleeves. "And the

funeral?" She rose to fill a Styrofoam cup with coffee. "Want some?"

"Here at 3:30 the day after tomorrow."

Jane handed Alberta a fresh cup of coffee. "Will there be any music?"

"Sam's doing it, I think. He's planning something classical."

Jane's eyes widened. "But Aggie never liked classical music."

"We both know that, but I don't think Sam does, and Teddy asked specifically for classical music."

Jane shook her head. "This is going to be some funeral."

Jane and Alberta stood in front of the funeral home chatting. "Is Teddy here yet?" asked Jane.

"I saw him going in just as I got here. A number of the congregation have already been in to pay their respects." Alberta straightened her scarf more closely around her throat. "I suppose we should go in too."

Jane shrugged. "I'm going in out of respect for Pastor Teddy."

"Me too," said Alberta. "From what I've overheard while I was waiting for you, that's the reason that most of the people came. She cut a wide swathe among the congregants over the years, I doubt that very many of them came because of her. I heard George say to his wife that he just wanted to make sure that she really was dead. Mary's as deaf as a post so he had to say it loudly."

Jane chuckled. "Trust George to tell it like it is."

"He went to school with her years ago, you know." Alberta pulled the heavy door to the funeral parlour open.

Jane stepped over the threshold. "That was before my time."

"I know, but he once told me that she was like a bear with a sore paw even in her younger days." Alberta unbuttoned her coat. "I heard after that that Aggie had jilted him years ago and he never got over it."

"Sh-sh," said Jane, "he'll hear you."

Alberta peeled her gloves off and got in line to sign the guest book. She glanced over the preceding signatures. "Hm, Jarrod is here already." She signed the guest book. "He didn't like her much either."

"Sh-sh," said Jane, "someone will hear you."

They followed the line going in to view Aggie and greet Pastor Teddy.

"Nice crowd," said Alberta. "I see you've been thoroughly kissed."

"Every woman in the church hath had a go," said Teddy. He mopped at his face with his cotton handkerchief.

"You'll need to do more than that before you go out in public."

Jane offered her hand to Pastor Teddy. "She looks good, doesn't she?"

The tiny smile came and went on Teddy's face. "They've done a wonderful job. She has never looked tho good."

Alberta looked at Teddy out the corner of her eye.

"You sound rather gleeful, Pastor Teddy. You'd better not say that too loudly."

Teddy pulled his face into more sober lines. "Of course, you're right, Mith Alberta. I have appreciated your rightness on many occasionth. I want you to know that."

Alberta raised one bushy eyebrow.

"It's true," said Teddy. "You've pulled me out of the fire more than once."

"Good evening, Mith Alberta—and the inevitable Mith Jane." A gleam of sarcasm sparkled briefly in Jarrod's eyes as he mocked Teddy.

Alberta rolled her eyes and moved on in the line. Jarrod followed. "She looks better than she ever has, don't you think?"

"She was never a raving beauty, if that's what you mean," said Alberta.

"Well, you would know," replied Jarrod. He turned away from the casket.

Alberta followed his progress across the room. "That

fellow needs his comeuppance." She turned to look at Aggie.

"He is right. She does look better than I've ever seen her, even in her youth." Alberta paused to look a few moments at Aggie.

"It took an army to fix her," said Molly. She sat among the flowers on the top of the casket and dangled her feet. "They were at it all day."

"Hm? Did you say something, Jane?" Alberta moved on in the line.

"Not a thing," said Jane. "This place is getting crowded, we need to move on."

"In a few minutes," said Alberta, "I want to visit with Grannie Banks, I haven't talked with her for a couple of weeks."

After the visitation was over the undertakers closed the lid of the casket to prepare for the service. Teddy mounted to the pulpit. "Dear friends." He gazed around at the congregation. "I have been so blessed to be part of your church these many years. It is a sad time for me, and I appreciate your support." He opened his Bible. "I want to read to you today from the book of Matthew." He began reading. His lisp had disappeared in the relief and solemnity of the occasion.

"My mother is gone now. She has been a part of my life all these years and it will take some time to realize what that will mean."

"It will mean, Teddy dear, that you are finally free," said Molly. She perched on the lowest rafter and straightened her black sequinned turban more firmly on her head. "I've never understood why people have to tell lies at funerals."

"Sh!" said Lucy. "We're not to speak ill of the dead."

"Why not? Some of them need to be spoken ill of." Molly smoothed the folds of her silver lame caftan over her knees. "It has been my experience that some people should be spoken ill of when they're alive. That way they can mend their ways before they die and save us a lot of time and energy doing it for them when they get here."

"Sh! Listen!"

"In the short term, it means I no longer have to worry about caring for her should she become incapacitated." Teddy regarded the congregation. "In the long term we will miss her.

"Speak for yourself," said Molly.

"Her interest in each of you who have known her since her childhood was vast."

"Nosy old biddy," said Molly.

"Will you please be quiet. Next thing you know someone will hear you," said Lucy.

"She was always ready with a word of encouragement," said Teddy.

"Humph! said Molly. "Like the time she encouraged old Mr. Carter into a heart attack."

"She was always the first one there when someone was ill," said Teddy.

"I heard about the time she went over to Miss Marian's and gave her shingles," said Molly.

"That was an accident," said Lucy. "Now be quiet."

"Some accident," said Molly. "Miss Marian was sick with the flu and her resistance was down and Aggie insisted that she change the dressing for her."

"In return for the casserole she brought her," said Lucy.

"Some casserole. She was suspicious that the sour cream was turned, but she used it anyway. Marian was laid up for another two weeks and between that and the flu, her husband almost died from it," said Molly.

"I'm sure many of you can remember the kindnesses that my mother has done for you over the years." Teddy paused and raised his eyes to the rafters. Molly waved at him. Teddy paled and swallowed hard.

"You're doing a fine job, Teddy," called Molly. "Keep it going."

Teddy clutched the edge of the pulpit and took a deep breath. "The many baby layettes she crocheted. The birthdays she remembered with a card."

"Humph!" said Molly. "I don't suppose you remember the layette she made for Linda's baby."

"Sh!" said Lucy.

"She was low on baby wool and made the sleeves and trim from carpet yarn. Poor wee thing broke out in a rash. It took her mother weeks to repair the damage," said Molly.

"The only reason she kept a birthday card list was so she could keep track of the people who were older than her, and the ones who were younger but had died before her." Molly fell silent for a moment. "I've seen her on many occasions gloating over her lists."

Lucy threw her hands in the air. "I can see you've done your homework."

"I always do," said Molly. "I check out the short term records as soon as I know I have an assignment. It's not safe to wing it."

"Mummy was a wonderful manager," said Teddy. He hazarded another glance toward the rafters. Molly waved again.

"I know we've all had reason to be thankful for her

skill with finances. In some ways she has had a wonderful influence on our young people."

Molly giggled outright. Teddy looked up at the rafters once more, then hastily looked down. "In conclusion, I hope each of you can carry a wonderful memory of Mummy with you. If anyone would like to share with us a happy encounter with Miss Aggie I will welcome you." Teddy closed his Bible and stepped down from the pulpit. No one came forward.

Teddy sighed softly.

Presently the funeral director and his assistant came forward to prepare the casket for transport. The pall bearers took their places and carried Miss Aggie to the waiting hearse. After a short drive, the hearse drew up in the cemetery near a fresh grave. Teddy began the committal service. The casket was slowly lowered into the rough box below.

"From dust we came; to dust we must return." Teddy dropped a handful of dirt into the grave.

Molly and Lucy had taken their places on the next

tombstone. "Ashes to ashes, dust to dust. If the Lord doesn't get you then the devil must," said Molly.

Chapter 12

"I'm going to lie low for the rest of the week, Miss Alberta." Teddy pulled on his overcoat. "Easter Pageant will be upon us soon, and I'd like to come to it feeling a little refreshed at least."

"Is there somewhere I can reach you if I need to?"

"I'll check in from time to time." Teddy picked up his battered briefcase. He lowered his voice. "Don't let Jarrod get to you if you can. Thank you for holding the fort once more." He turned and held the door for Jane who was about to enter. "Miss Jane, do come in. I won't be long away, Miss Alberta." The door whooshed to a close behind him.

"Wow! Are we changed or something?" Jane unbuttoned her coat and pulled her scarf away from her throat. "Where's he off to?"

Alberta pursed her lips. "I don't know, he wouldn't tell me. He just said he'd be in touch."

Jane poured coffee into two mugs and handed one to

Alberta. "There's something else changed about him. I can't quite put my finger on it." She frowned down into her cup.

"He seems taller somehow."

"I noticed that too," said Alberta. "I thought it was just my imagination. And you know, I haven't heard him lisp since the funeral. Is that possible?"

"I suppose so," said Jane. "It might depend on how bullied he felt by Aggie."

"You know, I believe you're right. If that's the case I'm looking forward to other changes. It'll be interesting to see how this turns out."

"Good day, Mith Alberta." Jarrod dropped a sheaf of papers on top of Alberta's work. "Ten copies collated by this evening, and hang the thign-up sheet on the main bulletin board."

"You can cut out the phony lisp any time, Jarrod. Pastor Teddy isn't here."

"Just trying to make you feel at home," said Jarrod. How long will he be gone for?"

"For the rest of the week. I assume he'll be back for Sunday."

Jarrod drew breath to respond to the information.

"And, no, Jarrod, he did not leave you in charge."

"Who'd he leave in charge?"

Alberta smiled sweetly. "Me."

Jarrod muttered something unpleasant and went back to his office.

"Hey, you're good, Alberta," said Jane. "You're a good second in command too."

"I should be after all these years." She began shuffling through the stack of papers Jarrod had left on her desk. "Hm, I guess this is the new revised standard version of the Easter Pageant." She picked up the sign-up sheet and glanced down the roles. "Fifteen parts, and most of them for women. I wonder how much the Disciples will have to say this year."

"He fancies himself a playwright too, does he?"

"You know he does." Alberta changed discs in her computer and began typing the sign up sheet. "I think this'll be a job for the Women's Union. We need to call a meeting."

"The Easter Pageant is still some time away, Alberta. We can go on as we have been going and continue to gum up the works with our unexplained absences. I don't think Jarrod has quite recovered from Christmas yet. Besides, we really didn't do a lot to spoil his ill-thought-out plans completely.

"Do we want to break him altogether, or just bend him a little?" asked Alberta.

"Break him, break him," chanted Molly from her seat on top of the file cabinet.

"Oh, Molly, that's just cruel," said Lucy from where she was sitting on the bookcase.

"Lucy, Jarrod is not a nice person and he deserves all he gets. He's mouthy, arrogant and a bully, especially to women. I think we should haunt him." Molly returned to her chanting. "Haunt him, haunt him."

"Right, Jane was saying, "it'll have to be an emergency meeting. We can set it for tomorrow evening."

"My place at seven-thirty," said Alberta.

Alberta pulled the loaf of monkey bread out of the oven and turned it upside down on the bread board. "This'll be cool enough to eat while we have our meeting." She pulled off her oven mitt just as the doorbell chimed. "Coming," she called.

"Come in everyone. We have a task to complete over Easter."

"What? Another boycott?" asked Maggie. She had greatly enjoyed the Christmas boycott and was sorry when it ended.

"We have the perfect opportunity. Jarrod just gave me the sign-up sheet for auditions for the Easter Pageant yesterday."

"Surely he must have caught on by now," said Grannie Banks.

"Does that mean we can't be in the Pageant this year?" asked Barbara Ann. "It seems a shame to spoil Easter Pageant too."

The ladies arranged themselves around Alberta's small kitchen and dining room.

"It's the only way we can make the male leaders appreciate how much we do around there," said Alberta. She poured coffee all around. "Here's what I think we should do." She set the cutting board with the fresh monkey bread in the middle of the table and pulled a large pat of Bordeaux butter from the refrigerator. "Jarrod wants the young girls to sign up for the auditions. I think we should make sure they can't."

"How'll we do that?" asked Barbara Ann. "It didn't work the last time."

"It did. Even better than we had hoped," said Grannie Banks. She pulled a piece of monkey bread off the loaf and buttered it generously. "Mmm, there's nothing like warm bread and butter. So what's the plan this time?"

Alberta added sweetener to her coffee and stirred. "I've been thinking about this ever since yesterday and I think we should all sign up for the choice roles. How about you auditioning for the Mary part,

Grannie Banks?"

Grannie licked the butter off her fingers. "I've always wanted to play Mary. That'll set a few old tongues wagging. I had a reputation when I was young."

"And Sandra, you sign up for the role of Mary Magdalene." Alberta passed the copy of the sign up sheet around the table. "I'll post the sheet on the bulletin board tomorrow."

"He hasn't left himself much time to prepare for this," said Maggie. "Six weeks to stage as big a production as he wants isn't much time.

"He never does," replied Alberta. "You just don't notice it because you're never in any of the plays."

"I'll keep the other girls from signing up," said Laurie. "They were more than a little put out with him over the Christmas Pageant."

"What'll Pastor Teddy have to say about this," asked Barbara Ann.

"I'm pretty sure he's on our side," said Alberta. "He doesn't like Jarrod much."

"Why didn't he do anything about him before this?" asked Maggie.

"He tried to when Jarrod first came here but Mummy interfered, and Jarrod has taken advantage over Pastor Teddy ever since." Alberta pulled a piece of bread from the loaf. "However, if I'm reading the signs correctly, that's about to change."

"Change how?" asked Lizzie. She mopped butter off her chin with great delicacy. "What do you know that we don't?"

"Just watch and wait," said Alberta. "I think this will be a rather exciting Easter Pageant."

"Can you put these notes into some kind of order, please, Miss Alberta? I will really appreciate it."

"Oh, Pastor Teddy, you're back." Alberta took the sheaf of notes and scanned through them. This will be an uplifting sermon or I miss my guess. Will you be staying now until Sunday?"

"I'm not back yet," said Teddy. "I'm still recovering

from Mummy's death. As difficult as she was, Mummy left quite a hole in my life."

"Are you staying at the house?"

"Tonight I am. I took a drive to the coast to think things over. A walk on the beach put everything in a different light."

"I'm sure it did," said Alberta.

"The matters were weighty and I had some serious decisions to make."

"You must have had the beach to yourself."

"It was heavenly. The wind was cold but not too cold to walk in. The sea had a greyish green colour to it. You know, it's a wintertime colour. The gulls were balancing in the breeze and crying to one another until a fishing boat motored past and they went to follow that. They're such scavengers." Teddy fell silent for a moment then said: "And now I have to go through Mummy's effects and decide what to do with it all. She was a terrible pack rat. I'll probably need a dumpster."

"D'you want some help?" Alberta clamped her mouth

shut at the audacity of her offer. "I'm sorry Pastor Teddy, that was very bold of me."

"Not at all," said Teddy. "I thank you for your offer. It's a very lonely job and I look forward to your presence. Why don't I order in something Chinese and we'll have a bite of supper before we start."

"Of course," said Alberta. "I'll come over as soon as I finish here."

"I'll see you a bit after five, then." Teddy stood up and buttoned his overcoat. "Until then." He pushed open the office door and disappeared into the gloom of the late afternoon light.

"I hope no one will observe this and take exception to it," said Alberta. "I've maintained my reputation for all these years, it would be a shame if I lost it all now." She settled herself on the floor and began sorting through a large box.

"Oh, Miss Alberta, I never even thought about that," said Teddy. "If you want to go, I'll understand."

"In for a penny, in for a pound, don't worry about it. I'm certainly not going to." Alberta pulled a tissue wrapped package from the box. "What in the world is this?" She unwrapped the piece. "A piece of wedding cake?" She lifted it to her nose and sniffed. "A tad musty but still a little moist."

"I can't believe Mummy would save that all these years."

"Surely it's not a piece of her own wedding cake."

"I think so," replied Teddy. "I know she did have one so I suppose this must be it. Though why she saved it all this time is beyond me. She didn't have a good word to say about Daddy and they married at least fifty years ago."

"I guess it wouldn't be safe to eat now, would it?"

Teddy shuddered. "I don't think so, Miss Alberta. Dear knows what kind of germs are breeding in there."

Alberta tossed it into the waste basket beside her. She rummaged in silence for a few minutes. Presently she said: "What's this?" She unwrapped a piece of pink cloth surrounding a lumpy object and stared at the object in wonder for a moment or two. "I can't believe she saved this."

Teddy looked over from the box he was sorting through. "What is it?"

Alberta held it up to the light. "It's an old breast pump. But why the pink cover?" She turned the pump back and forth in her hands.

"Mummy was always afraid people would find fault with her over this. I was a fraternal twin. The other baby was a girl and stayed in hospital for most of her short life. Mummy had to pump milk for her and carry it to the hospital every day."

"I never knew that," said Alberta. "Why would she fear what people would say? She was certainly never afraid of what people thought lately. In any case, how do you know all this?"

"I heard the story when I was about thirteen from a friend of mine who heard it from his mother. He swore me to secrecy. He thought he'd get a licking for repeating it to me. I didn't believe it anyway, until one day I was rummaging around in the attic and I found Mummy's old diary from when she was first married and read about it. It told everything down to the unpleasant details, and she swore that she'd never have another child."

"I guess I wouldn't blame her," said Alberta. "But I still don't understand why. She should have been supported by the community, not put down."

"Her family thought she'd married beneath her, and the babies came too soon after the marriage." Teddy sighed. "I think that was part of the reason she was so unpleasant with the younger girls. She was very critical of them no matter what they did, and if one made a mistake, as she called it, she was very down on her."

"How sad. I guess that sheds some light on some of her obnoxious behaviour." Alberta picked up a sheaf of old cards and letters. "I suppose there are her wedding cards."

Teddy glanced across to see what Alberta was holding.

"Actually those are both wedding cards and cards of congratulations on the birth of her babies. The one edged in black is a sympathy card when the other baby died."

"It doesn't seem as if the community was against her."

"No, she just thought they were. She became very melancholy after that and she just kept getting worse. She was hard on my father, so much so that he finally left."

"D'you suppose she was suffering from untreated depression all these years?" Alberta rifled through the stack of cards.

"She might have been. I know she was always unpleasant, and it seemed that no matter what I did, I couldn't please her." Teddy hitched himself onto the edge of the bed. I found her looking through these a few years ago, and I think she was crying. She didn't like it that I had caught her and she covered up pretty quickly."

Alberta held up the stack of cards. "Trash or keep?"

"Trash, I think. I've seen them all once and it really

was her tragedy, not mine."

"And it didn't need to be a tragedy at all."

Teddy picked up his empty box and hurled it into the hall. "I'll get that later." He pulled another box out of the closet. "This is the last box, I think, except for a few in the attic. If you're not too tired I'd like to go through her clothes and see what to keep for the donation box and what to throw away."

Decisions on the fate of Aggie's apparel were quickly made. Alberta looked at her watch. "Good heavens! D'you know what time it is? I'd better get going or people will really be talking."

"Where were you last evening?" asked Jane.

Alberta arched her furry eyebrows. "That's for me to know and you to find out."

"I'm trying in my own simple way," replied Jane. "Now, tell me."

"Between you and me?"

"Always."

Alberta lowered her voice almost to a whisper. "I was helping Pastor Teddy go through Aggie's things. There was more to Aggie than we ever imagined."

"Bless my soul," said Jane. "He must be back, then."

"Who's back? And what are you two whispering about?" Jarrod's freckled face came around the corner of the door. The rest of him soon followed. "Have you posted the sign-up sheet like I asked you to?"

"None of your business, and none of your business, and I posted it yesterday before I went home."

"Have you looked at it yet?"

"No. I haven't had time. Besides that's your project." Jarrod went out the door and around the corner to where the sign up sheet was posted. A bellow of rage filled the hallway and penetrated the office. Jarrod stormed back into the office waving the sheet. "Who did this?" He waved the crumpled sign up in Alberta's face.

"Did what" Alberta tore the list from Jarrod's sweaty grasp. She scanned down the list. "I see Barbara Ann has volunteered to be an angel again." She handed the sheet back to Jarrod. "So what's wrong with this list? The roles have people of character offering for them."

"They're all old," Jarrod snarled. "I cannot and will not have old women playing the girls' parts."

Alberta chewed on her upper lip to prevent a smile escaping. "I guess you'd better get busy recruiting, hmm?"

Jarrod scowled at Alberta. "You're behind this aren't you?" His face got redder. "In fact, you were behind the Christmas program too."

"As a matter of fact, I wasn't. I was just an interested bystander."Alberta watched Jarrod's complexion turn almost purple. "Take a deep breath, Jarrod, you're liable to pop a freckle."

Another snarl of impotent rage issued from Jarrod. He turned on his heel and went back to his office. In a moment the sound of his door slamming echoed down the hall.

"Wow! I've never seen him in such a rage," said Jane. "I hope he's alright. It wouldn't look good if we had to report another stroke victim at the Church of the Misbegotten."

Alberta shrugged. "He'll be okay, he's young. I suppose I'd better post another list and see what comes of it. After that I'm calling it done for the day. "Want to go somewhere for supper?"

"I can't." said Jane "I have papers to grade and if the writing is as bad as it was the last time, it'll be midnight before I'm done." She crossed her scarf across her chest and shrugged her coat into place on her shoulders. "Maybe Pastor Teddy'll take you out." Her eyes sparkled. "You can tell me all about it tomorrow."

"I doubt he will" said Alberta, "and if he does I should really say no, because people will start to notice, and with something like that it doesn't take long for rumours to start."

"Suit yourself," replied Jane,"he's actually kind of cute."

Cute, my foot. thought Alberta. He hasn't been cute

since he was in diapers. He's plump and balding. His ruddiness is such that he always looks as if he's about ready to have a stroke. I heard that those run in families. Her thoughts wandered on. But he's kind and thoughtful, and now that he's on the wagon, he's more present in his life. She leaned her head on her hands and pursed her lips. It sure makes it easier for me since he's been taking control around here. She sat upright and shook her head. I've got to stop thinking like that. The next thing I know I'll be finding him cute too.

The outer door whooshed open and then shut letting in a wave of cold spring air. Alberta looked up.

"I see you're still here, Miss Alberta." Pastor Teddy set his briefcase on the floor and dropped into one of the moulded chairs. "Are you always this late leaving?"

Alberta scooped the papers she had been working on into a bundle and squared the stack on the edge of her desk. She looked at her watch. "I'm always a little late leaving. Jarrod usually wants everything yesterday."

"Next time, send him to me and I'll deal with him."

Alberta's bushy eyebrows twitched. "I'll do that," she said.

"Is there anything I can do to help you now to get ready to go home?"

"As a matter of fact, you can hang this list on the bulletin board in the hall." She selected Jarrod's revised version of the pageant role list. "I haven't had a chance."

Pastor Teddy glanced over the list. "I thought you'd already posted this list. I'm sure I saw the list the other day, and it was filled."

Alberta shrugged. "Jarrod didn't like the ladies who signed up."

"I'll have a word with him about this. He can't exclude all these people even though he wants to."

"I'm glad it's you and not me." Alberta sighed. "I've had enough guff from him these last five years to last me the rest of my life."

"Why didn't you tell me?"

"I tried to on several occasions, but Aggie interfered. Besides, you weren't really here those days."

"I know, and I'm sorry to have been such a burden to you and a few of the others who have helped me all these years." It was Teddy's turn to sigh. "There are some really solid people in this church. I must make amends with everyone once I get my act together again," He began buttoning his coat. "And you'll be the first one."

Alberta shook her head. "Don't fret about that, Pastor Teddy, I don't hold grudges and I'm more than happy to see you pulling yourself together."

Chapter 13

"Miss Alberta, where might I find a copy of the budget from last year?" Pastor Teddy waved a sheaf of papers around in the air. "I can only find this one and it's from year before last."

"I have it here." said Alberta. "It was kind of a mess so I copied out a new one and I put it in the top drawer of my filing cabinet because I couldn't find where you'd put the others. I thought I should keep an extra copy for myself."

"Once again I find myself indebted to you." said Pastor Teddy. "The planning committee has run aground financially, and I couldn't figure out where I'd put it. It took me all morning to find the others."

Alberta rummaged in the top drawer of her filing cabinet and pulled out the report. "I believe this will make your collection complete. She handed him the report.

"Thank you. Miss Alberta. I'll be more accountable in the future." He turned and walked straight down the hall to his office, never missing a step.

That's the first time I've seen him do that in years, thought Alberta. His personality is changing for the better too.

Jarrod poked his head around the door and thrust another handful of papers at Alberta. "I want these by noon."

"I suppose you don't mean noon tomorrow." Alberta peered at him from over the edge of her glasses.

"No. I don't. And not next week either," said Jarrod. "I want them by noon today."

"How'd I ever guess?" Alberta rolled her eyes.

"You're out of line, Alberta. Today, Mith Alberta, or I'll report this to the powers that be as insubordination."

"And who might those be?" Alberta picked up the papers as if they were dirty. "Play manuscripts?" She turned the papers around to see them better. "I just typed these yesterday and I'm not going over them again." She handed the pages back to Jarrod who let them shower over the floor.

"Pick those up." Jarrod's face became ever more red.

Alberta shrugged. "They're your papers. Pick them up yourself." She returned to her work on Teddy's sermon.

"You look at me when I'm speaking to you." His voice rose to a squeak.

Alberta sighed and turned her attention back to Jarrod. "You'd better watch that nasty temper, Jarrod. You look as if you're going to pop a blood vessel." Alberta sat with her hands folded and waited for Jarrod to speak.

Jarrod took a breath. "This is the last straw, Miss Alberta. I'm reporting you." He turned and stomped toward his office. Presently his door slammed.

"Amen," said Alberta softly. The outer door whooshed open.

"Amen to what?" asked Jane.

"I told Jarrod that I couldn't type his manuscript and he's going to report me to the powers that be."

"Who does he imagine are these powers?" Jane opened her coat and slipped out of it.

"I suppose he thinks the elders will listen to him." said Alberta.

"They'll just pass it on to Teddy, won't they?"

Alberta rolled her shoulders to ease an incipient ache. "Of course, they will. And Teddy will pass it back to me."

"So I suppose, that leaves you as the main power that is."

"Right you are." Alberta sat up straighter and stretched her arms behind her head. "I'd offer you coffee but the pot is almost gone, and I didn't plan to make anymore this morning."

"That's okay, I wasn't going to stay." Jane shrugged into her coat. "I just wanted to come by and see how the battle was going."

"That's okay, you saw." The phone rang. Alberta picked up the receiver. "Yes, Pastor Teddy." Alberta listened for a moment. "I'll find it for you. Just don't touch anything. and I'll bring my note pad." She hung up the phone and shuffled through the pages of Teddy's sermon. "I don't know what's going on, but he asked me to take notes." She stuck her pencil into the sharpener.

"Must be serious," said Jane. She lifted on eyebrow. "I'll want a complete report on my desk yesterday."

"Grr," said Alberta. She went down the hall and tapped lightly on Teddy's door.

"Come in Miss Alberta." Teddy pulled the blotter off his desk and shuttled through the debris that lay under in it. "I know I put it somewhere, I was only reading it last week."

"What are you looking for? I might know where to find it."

"I made notes on a project I was thinking about presenting to the board of trustees." He set the blotter on edge and leaned it against the desk. It began a slow slide to the floor and stopped at Alberta's feet. She bent to pick it up.

"Is this what you're looking for?" She lifted the blotter out of its leather holder and pulled out a thin bundle from behind the mat.

"Bless you. Miss Alberta. I don't know what I'd do without you."

Alberta raised her bushy eyebrows and peered at Teddy over the top of her glasses. "You'd get along just fine, I'm sure."

"Do you really think so?" He shuffled the sheets of paper into order and handed them to Alberta. "I want you to skim these now and tell me what you think. Do sit down and make yourself comfortable."

Alberta sat down on the edge of the sofa. "Hm." she said. She frowned and turned the page over. "Hm," she said again. She finished reading and then sat mulling over the information for a few moments.

"Well," asked Teddy. "D'you like it?"

"Yes. I think I do. It'll be a lot of work and will take some time to carry it out." She fell silent and thought some more. She nodded. "Yes, I do like it. If you can keep you know who out of the loop just now, I think it'll work. It's certain that we've needed something like this for quite some time."

Teddy's face crinkled into a broad grin. "I'm glad, Miss Alberta. If I may, I'd like to put you in charge of the undertaking of the plan. You work well with the board of trustees and I'm going to need all the help I can get."

"Thank you for your vote of confidence, Pastor Teddy. We've needed to do something about the structure of power and who does what within it for a long time now." Alberta skimmed the first page again. She frowned. "Why all of a sudden like this?"

"I've wanted to do it for years, but I couldn't."

"Mummy?"

Teddy nodded. "And a few other things. I ran the idea by Mummy once and she pooh poohed it. And, of course, with everything else it didn't get done."

Alberta nodded in sympathy. "Aggie really ran this place, didn't she."

"With a rod of iron." Teddy leaned his head back against his chair and closed his eyes. "She was always so scornful."

"Well, I think it's a grand plan, and I'll be more than

glad to help you. When do we start?"

Teddy sat up and straightened his tie. "I'd like to start as soon as possible. If you will kindly copy these notes we can start right now."

"I can do that, but I still need to finish on your sermon for Sunday."

"Don't fret about that. I've been over it so many times I can practically recite it from memory. Can you spare an hour just now?"

Alberta came back with a copy for herself and a new copy for Teddy. Teddy had pulled the wing chair into place across the desk from his own. "That didn't take you long."

"I managed to evade Jarrod for once." She laid the copies of the notes on the desk and settled into the wing chair with her notepad and pencil.

Teddy sat down opposite her and folded his chubby hands. "I think we need to brainstorm a little." He pursed his lips. "I'm wondering if an increased church maintenance budget is in order. The last time I asked for one, Mummy vetoed it.

"Why?"

"She liked to manage." Teddy picked up a pen and pulled off the cap. "This is what I've been thinking." Teddy began to write and draw on his legal pad. "I think if we begin with Ed Young and put him in the leadership of the elders he can perhaps stir the others on to achieving my goals." He passed the page to Alberta.

"We need to establish who's the boss. Mr. Young is a relative newcomer here. Won't the others resent his taking over?"

"I trust that with proper preparation they won't be too hurt or angry. After all, they're all getting on in years. Most of them are well past retirement. I was talking to George Misner a couple of days ago and he sounded more than eager to step down."

"He's been here almost from the beginning. He's done a lot for this place." Alberta filled in Mr. Misner's name.

"I know. He's carried most of the burden of the

church on his shoulders." Teddy sat silently for a few moments, then said: "I asked Mr. Young if he would be willing to take on the job and he was more than eager. He has a fund of ideas on what needs to be done here."

"What will the others say?" Alberta made another note on her pad. "Most of them are George's age."

"I've already talked to most of them, and we'll be having a meeting with them the next time they have one."

Alberta picked up the small desk calendar and ran her finger down the weeks. "They should be having one next week." She set the calendar back on the desk. "By the way, Pastor Teddy, who did you mean when you said 'we'?"

Teddy blinked and thought for a moment. "Why, you and I. Who else would I mean?"

Alberta shrugged. "Jarrod is your associate pastor."

"He might not be here by then."

Alberta sat forward on her chair, alert and curious. "What do you mean?"

"I heard how rude he was being to you a few minutes ago. That cannot go on. Has he always been this rude to you?"

Alberta nodded then sat staring down at her hands. "As soon as he got the lay of the land, and he's been getting worse over the years." She looked at Teddy over the rim of her glasses. "I expect he discerned early on that you wouldn't do anything about it." She stared down at her hands again.

Teddy sat silently for a few minutes. Alberta peeked at him again. Teddy shook his head. "It was that bad, was it?"

"Yes," said Alberta. "It was."

"What have I done?" said Teddy softly. He looked across the desk at Alberta's bowed head. "And you bore the brunt of it."

Alberta nodded. "It was worse when your mother was around because he knew he had her support."

"Why didn't you say something?"

Alberta shrugged. "I knew it wouldn't make much

difference. That you'd have forgotten it by the time you got back to your office."

Teddy reached across the desk and patted Alberta's hand. "Can I ever make it up to you?" He sat and scrutinized the top of Alberta's bowed head.

"I doubt it," said Alberta, "but it's water under the bridge now." She rolled her shoulders to ease the ache in them. "You need to go forward with your plan, whatever that is."

Teddy sat back in his chair and thought for a moment. "You know Miss Alberta, despite what those on the board think, you and I are the most senior members of this congregation. The others have just dropped in along the way. Most of them came from the old church. So what better way to celebrate this dubious honour than to name you as my second in command, and solicit you for ideas for this church? What do you think needs to happen here to recreate a viable church?" He folded his arms across his chest as he waited for Alberta's thoughts on the subject.

Alberta wrote a list rapidly, then sat up and handed the list to Teddy. "There's what I think needs to be done, and in this order."

"That was fast." Teddy scanned down the list. "There's a lot of general maintenance things to do, and cleaning. The bell tower needs to be repaired, and the whole place needs painting inside and out. New carpets, wobbly pews. You have quite a list here, Miss Alberta." He glanced over the list once more.

"What's wrong with the bell tower?"

Alberta shrugged. "It was hit by lightening a few years ago and has been leaking ever since. That's why the ceiling in this room is discoloured."

"Where was I?"

"Someplace else in the building, I guess. Wherever you were you didn't get hurt and never mentioned anything about it. Ed Young and George Misner went up on the roof to check out the damage and thought there wasn't any and so they didn't have any reason to do anything about it. The next heavy rain we had, your ceiling started to drip and hasn't stopped since." Alberta stopped talking.

Teddy shook his head. "What a dreadful excuse for a pastor I've been. It's a wonder that I wasn't let go."

"No one would have said anything. They were your friends." Alberta straightened and looked Teddy in the eyes. "So was I."

Teddy looked long into Alberta's eyes, then sighed. "You too, Miss Alberta?"

Alberta's glance never wavered. She nodded. "Me too."

Teddy closed his eyes and sat back in his chair. "What other sins have I perpetrated on you and the others?"

Alberta sat up straighter in her chair. "You're addressing most of them in this new plan. Over the years I've asked you for most of this stuff but you never carried out any of it." She squared her shoulders. "In any case, it's all over now. We just need to get these things past planning and maintenance."

They worked on the structure of the undertaking for the rest of the day, not even stopping for lunch. Jarrod's leave taking was emphasized by the slamming of the door which neither of them heard. The early spring darkness filtered into the office until Alberta stretched and rubbed her eyes. "It's already dark out. I didn't realize how late it was getting. I told Jane I'd call her this evening." She gathered up her papers. "I'll put these in some kind of order tomorrow and get them copied. By the way, we could use a new copier."

Teddy rose. "Put it on the list." He stretched his shoulders. "I'm sorry that I've kept you so long."

Alberta's eyes sparkled. "Think nothing of it. I like this kind of challenge."

"You still haven't time to get these typed, Miss Alberta?" Jarrod waved his manuscript at Alberta.

"You're going to have to do your own typing for awhile. After all, that's what you have a typewriter for." She returned her attention to her task.

Jarrod's flat hand came down hard on the desk beside Alberta. "Miss Alberta." Jarrod lost his mocking lisp. "I've been keeping track of our encounters for the last year or so, and insubordination is written clearly across every one."

Alberta looked up from her task. "Look, Jarrod, I have work to do for Pastor Teddy, and until that's done I don't have time for anything else." She returned to her work.

"Pastor Teddy's gofer girl," muttered Jarrod. The door to his office slammed hard enough to skew the pictures on Alberta's wall.

"I have all this done and organized into a file for each of the elders." Alberta tapped them on the edge of the desk to square them.

"You're a marvel of enterprise," said Teddy. "I hope you know how valuable you are."

Alberta blushed and ducked her head. "I am, after all, just a secretary." The blush subsided. "I've had good training in office skills." She cleared her throat.

"Nevertheless, I appreciate all your good work." Teddy turned on his heel. He called back over his shoulder. "That meeting will be a couple of hours at least, why don't you take the rest of the afternoon off, go shopping or something."

Alberta thumped down on her chair and looked after Teddy. "Well, I never," she muttered. "What in the world has come over you?"

"Good, you're here, Miss Alberta." Jarrod tossed the play manuscript down in front of Alberta.

Alberta looked up at Jarrod staring at him as if she'd never seen him before.

"Was Pastor Teddy coming unglued again?" Jarrod poked a bony finger at the manuscript laying in front of Alberta. "I need these by tomorrow morning."

Alberta came to herself again. She stood up and started putting on her coat. "Too late, Jarrod. I've been working evenings these past few days and I'm taking the rest of the day off. There's the elders' meeting this evening."

Jarrod sniffed. "And I suppose you have to be here for that?" Jarrod picked up his papers and returned to his office.

"I'm glad this isn't the dead of winter," said Jane. She uncurled herself on the veranda swing. "I'd have frozen before now. Where have you been all afternoon?"

Alberta rooted in her left coat pocket for her keys. "Shopping. Come in and let me tell you about it."

Alberta stood aside to let Jane to enter. Jane slid out of her coat and flung it over the back of the wicker rocking chair. Alberta peeled out of her boots and coat and put them in their appointed places.

"The kitchen's cozier. Come on back."

"So what's your excuse?" asked Jane.

"Teddy gave me the afternoon off so I used it wisely. He told me to go and buy myself some dresses, so I did. Jarrod was foaming at the mouth about it. As usual he wanted something last week and I refused to do it for him. I told him I'd probably have time tomorrow and that if he wanted it any faster than that he'd have to do it himself." Alberta sat down in her father's old armchair and pulled a pair of sock slippers over her feet. "Mm, that feels better already."

Jane sat down on the couch and tucked her feet underneath herself. "So, give, what's going on?" She folded her hands in her lap.

Alberta propped her feet on the ottoman and leaned back into the curves that her father's body had worn into it. "I'd been working hard this past week, lots of overtime, so Teddy recognized that and told me to take the rest of the day off. I have to go back for the elders' meeting tonight. That's all."

"That's more than kind of him, isn't it?" Jane tucked her hands more firmly into her elbows. "What do you make of it?"

"I think he really is off the sauce and becoming more and more alert to the business of running a church.

What do you think of it?"

Jane folded her hands in her lap again. "You're probably right. Not having known Teddy for as long you have I don't think I can fairly make a judgment."

"So what's your news? You're looking all sparkly this evening." Alberta watched Jane's changing expression. "C'mon, spill it."

Jane giggled a tiny giggle and sparkled even more. She pulled her left hand out of her lap and stuck it out for Alberta to see. "There it is."

Alberta gasped. "Wow! When and where did you get that?" She pulled Jane's hand toward herself to better see the diamond.

"Yesterday evening at dinner. I was totally surprised. I never knew that was what he had in mind."

"He, who, Sam?"

Jane blushed. "Of course, Sam. Who else have I been seeing these past few months?"

"I'm sorry, Jane, all I've been able to do these last weeks is work, and avoid Jarrod. I'm quite adept at it." She pulled Jane's hand closer for another look. "My goodness, that is a pretty ring." She nodded her approval. "Have you set the date yet?"

"May, I think. I don't want to be a June bride, it's too trite. Sam agrees with that. I want you to be my matron of honour."

"This is so sudden I can hardly believe it. Congratulations! And of course, I'll be your matron of honour."

Chapter 14

Alberta laid a manila folder in front of each place on the meeting room table. The coffee urn gurgled on a side table. "It seems darker in here than usual. Does it seem that way to you?" She picked up the water pitcher and inspected it for dust.

Teddy looked up at the central lighting fixture. "There are several bulbs out. Do we have any more?"

"I'll have to look." Alberta stuck her hand into the wide mouth of the pitcher and picked out a dead fly and a dust bunny. "I'll have to wash this before we use it. I just hope we have some ice cubes."

"Put that on the list too."

"Put that on the list too, Mith Alberta." Jarrod's sniping tones were not hard to identify.

"What're you doing here, Jarrod?" Alberta held the dusty pitcher close to her chest.

"Why, Mith Alberta, I heard there was a meetin' here tonight." Jarrod looked down his nose at Alberta. "And you can guess what for."

Alberta suppressed an unladylike grunt. "I suppose you're here to complain about me."

"You got it, Mith Alberta." Jarrod sat down on the head chair and laid an untidy sheaf of papers in front of himself.

Teddy came out from behind the door where he had been sorting through his own papers to get them in order. "What are you doing here, Jarrod?"

"I came to talk to the elders. I guess that can't be indictable, Pastor Teddy." Jarrod's half smile turned into a grin and he giggled.

"I see. I don't suppose you're aware of the proper procedure to address the board of elders?" Teddy firmed his lips into a straight line.

"I didn't know there was one. In any case, the item I want to discuss will only take five minutes." Jarrod opened his folder and began leafing through his papers.

"Nevertheless, Jarrod, you can't just arrive at a meeting of the elders and expect to be heard. If you will follow the procedure I'm sure we can get you on the agenda for next month."

Jarrod's face turned scarlet. His freckles looked as if they were about to explode. "I suppose you know what I was going to bring up and are trying to block it."

"I have no idea," said Teddy.

"I wrote up a complaint about Miss Alberta and her insubordination these days. I think she's slipping into early dementia. She is constantly rude and dismissive of all my projects. In short, I think she is an abominable receptionist and not worthy of her place on the staff." Jarrod's lips turned into a sneer, and his freckles faded to pale polka dots.

Teddy's face turned white; his eyes grew dark with anger. "This is the last straw, Jarrod. You've been rude and harassing of Miss Alberta ever since you came here, and I'll not have it anymore. You're not welcome at this meeting, and I, for one, will be obliged if you pick up your papers and leave."

"You'll not have it," said Jarrod. "You and Miss

Alberta are in league with one another and have always been. It's a conspiracy. She's only good for drinking coffee and gossiping with her friends."

Teddy's face went whiter still. He stood over Jarrod and braced his chubby hands on the desk beside him. "You're done. I expect your office to be cleared out by the end of the week."

Jarrod got to his feet and gathered up his papers. "You can't fire me. I was taken on by the board of elders and they won't look well on this."

Alberta sighed. "Why don't you just go quietly, Jarrod. You'll be happier elsewhere, and you won't have to put up with me."

"That's true, Mith Alberta, I won't have to deal with you every day. Your boyfriend will have you all to himself. Cootchy coo." Jarrod turned to leave. Teddy blocked his way.

"You are to apologize to Miss Alberta. She is one of the many fine people who have dedicated themselves to the welfare of this church."

Jarrod lost all composure. "I'll do no such thing. She's nothing but a common tart. Having cozy dinners for two at her house. Waiting in her ruffled apron for Pastor Teddy to come home. How do we know that she isn't secretly living with you and ...."

"And what, Jarrod?" Alberta spoke for the first time in the argument. "What is it I have supposedly done? Be kind to a fellow human being when his mother has just died?"

"Having a secret affair."

"You will apologize to Miss Alberta," said Teddy. "She is one of the finest woman ever given breath. She and I have been through our whole lives together from the first day of school. She is the woman whom I will marry."

Alberta's eyebrows almost disappeared up under her hair. She opened her mouth to speak but no words came out. She stood immobilized with her mouth agape.

Teddy's face had developed into a blush that even coloured his bald spot. "By Friday," he said. "You'll be able to get everything done if you start now. In the meantime, you can leave your complaints about Miss Alberta on my desk."

"Good evening, Pastor." George Misner pushed his businessman's bulk into the room. "What's the scoop? Why's Jarrod here looking so discomposed?"

Ed arrived on a blast of early spring air from the outside door. "I could hear you guys in the parking lot."

"You probably could," said Teddy. His blush had faded to his normal pink. "I was trying to help Jarrod understand the rules of presenting a case to the elders. He's not a fast learner."

"I've known that for some time," said Ed. "What does he not understand?"

Teddy sighed. "Many things, most of them in the areas of being human."

Jarrod snorted. "Pastor Teddy has relieved me of my duties. He says I'm to be gone by Friday. What's your word on it?"

George was silent for a moment. "I expect he has

reason for it. I trust his decisions."

Jarrod turned toward Ed.

"Don't look at me," said Ed. "I've known Teddy since first grade and he has always had a reason, no matter how obscure the reasoning. I trust him."

"We'll arrange an exit interview for Thursday evening," said George. "Then you can complain all you want."

"The others are arriving," said Ed. "It's time you left, Jarrod."

Jarrod turned on his heels and shouldered his way through the group of men who were hanging up their coats on the rack.

Herbie Masters was the first one into the meeting room. "What's with Jarrod? He's in an awful mood."

The rest of the elders filed into the meeting room and found their places.

"The problem with Jarrod," said Teddy, "is that I fired him." Teddy gazed around the room. "He has been rude and insufferable to Miss Alberta, and unkind and disrespectful to almost all the other women in the church."

"None too soon," said George. "I, for one, don't know how he managed to stay here for so long."

"That was my fault," said Teddy, "and I want to apologize to all of you for my failings over these past few years. I know now what a trial I must have been to everyone."

Alberta had taken a chair at the side desk. Teddy turned to her. "Miss Alberta, come and take your rightful place at this table."

"This is fine for me," said Alberta.

"I've been doing some serious thinking and you're a part of it, Miss Alberta."

Alberta gathered up her pad and pencils. Ed made room for her between him and George.

Teddy cleared his throat. "Miss Alberta and I have been doing some brain storming. If you'll look in your folders you'll see the framework of our plan. These are only preliminary and I do want your thoughts on them. Ultimately, I hope to move Miss Alberta to executive secretary in charge of this program. As you can see, we'll need to do a number of repairs and maintenance jobs. We can hire them out or they can be done by volunteers from the congregation. I'll give you a few minutes to look things over."

"With Miss Alberta taking a leadership role, won't we have to hire a replacement for her so she won't get bogged down in the business of answering the phones and all the other things she does here?" Ed's pencil moved quickly across the paper.

Teddy nodded. "You're right. Shall we offer it as a minimum wage job to the congregation?"

"We could put it out there and see who comes forward," said Thomas. "How soon do you want to implement these plans?"

"As soon as we can," said Teddy. "I'll need agreement from each of you. Feel free to make suggestions. I think the common housekeeping chores should take place regardless of whatever else we do."

"One of the first things we should do is repair that steeple," said Stan. "It's a wonder that it's still up there and not falling around our ears."

"We'll have to hire that done," said Harry. "We can't afford to have one of our own up there taking a wrong step from inexperience and falling off. It's a very high steeple."

"Besides," said Ed, "our insurance wouldn't cover that."

"Yeah," said Stan, "I was looking at the agreement the other day and it will only cover insured professionals."

Alberta scribbled in her note book. At a pause in the discussion she said: "Pastor Teddy's office needs some attention where the leak from the steeple got through."

"We'll see to that too," said Ed. "Doesn't Paul Schneider own a construction company?"

"Haven't seen him lately," said Harry. "He hasn't been ushering since a long while."

Alberta's pencil paused. "He has moved his membership over to St. James." Her pencil began scurrying across the pad again. "He hasn't been here since a year ago August."

"That long?" said Ed.

"I ran into him the other day at the hardware store," said Harry. "I asked him how things were going. He said, much better, then he asked me if things were still the same here."

"Did he say why he left?" asked Teddy.

"Not specifically. He alluded to Jarrod and his cronies but didn't expand on the subject. We left it like that."

"He's a good singer. He left an enormous hole in the choir when he left," said Teddy. "He's a true bass. It's a shame to let him get away like that. I've known him since before kindergarten."

"Perhaps you should go talk to him, Pastor Teddy," said George. "He'll probably be glad you did, and you never know, you might entice him to come back."

"It might just be the catalyst he needs. He was brought up in this church. I met him in Sunday school."

Alberta paused her scribbling long enough to ask: "Shall I contact him for this?"

Teddy helped Alberta into her coat. "Wrap your scarf around, you don't want to catch cold," he said.

Alberta buttoned her coat and picked up her purse. "Thank you, Pastor Teddy. I'll see you in the morning."

"I'll walk you to your car." He held the door for her. "We got a fine lot of work done this evening, don't you think?"

"I'm impressed," said Alberta. "I was afraid no one would want to start a repair project, it has been so long since anything was done."

Teddy moved his briefcase to his other hand and held the outside door for Alberta. "I don't know why Aggie was so adamant against routine repairs. I would have thought that would be in her interests to keep the building in shape."

"It wasn't that she was so against repairs," said Alberta. "It was because she didn't want to go through me to accomplish her goals."

"How strange," said Teddy. "I guess I didn't know the half of what she was up to, or not up to." He took

Alberta's car keys from her gloved hand and unlocked the car door.

"Thank you, Teddy." Alberta threw her note pad on the passenger seat, then turned. "Did you mean what you said?"

"Hush, Alberta, it's almost midnight. We'll talk about this tomorrow." Teddy lifted Alberta's gloved hand to his lips in a gallant gesture. "Until tomorrow. Sleep well."

Alberta went home to a cool house and a somewhat sleepless night. She picked up the telephone receiver to call Jane, then put it down again. I can't talk to Jane about this. It's Teddy's and my business, she thought. Besides, it's late. She turned up the heat and hung her coat on the rack in the hall. She closed the kitchen door to better retain the heat from the furnace.

I wish I could talk to Jane. She filled the kettle and set it on the stove to boil. No, I'm right, it's no one's business except mine and Teddy's. She pulled off her shoes and stuck her feet into her slippers. But I need to talk to someone.

The kettle whistled. She poured the boiling water over the powdered chocolate in her big mug and stirred it to dissolve the grains. She reached for the telephone one more time. No! I'll not call Jane, at least not tonight. She'll be asleep by now anyway. She set her mug on the side table by her father's recliner and curled her legs under herself. She warmed her hands on the mug. I wish I could talk to Daddy about it all. Would he approve of Teddy? Do I approve of Teddy? He's making a serious turnaround in his life, but can I trust him to continue in his sobriety? It would be a terrible thing to be locked into marriage with him and have him go back to his old ways. She pulled the lap robe over herself and sipped at her chocolate. There's no way of knowing, either.

"Humph" said Molly, "she can always talk to me." Molly and Lucy were sitting side by side on the sofa across from Alberta.

"You haven't exactly been available lately," said Lucy. "ever since you and Larry got together you've only been here half the time."

"Well, I'm here now." Molly scowled at the idea that she may have done something wrong. "I'm always where I'm supposed to be. I keep tabs on what's going on."

"So you know that Jarrod's gone."

"Of course I do. I also know about you and that good looking newcomer."

Lucy blushed as only a spirit can—an off shade of pink. "I knew him in high school."

"Be that as it may," said Molly. "He's here now so what are you going to do about it?"

"He's a friend," said Lucy. "Don't you think you'd better stick with the business at hand?"

"Humph," said Molly. She pondered her next move for a moment. She looked across at Alberta sitting in her father's chair and wearing his old sweater for comfort. "Hello, Bertie." It was a childhood nickname given to her by her father. "Oh, Bertie, pay attention. You did say you wanted someone to talk to."

Alberta shook her head as if to clear it.

"You're not imagining things," said Molly. "And you are quite sane, despite today's events."

"Daddy?" Alberta looked worried. "Is that you?"

"I'm not your father," said Molly. "Now, pay attention."

Alberta pulled her legs from underneath herself and sat up straight.

"You said you wanted someone to talk this over with, didn't you?"

"Yes," quavered Alberta.

"So talk," said Molly.

"Pastor Teddy practically proposed to me in front of Jarrod this afternoon and I don't know what to say."

"Say yes," said Molly. "You've certainly known him long enough. You know he's an upright and good man. There's nothing holding him back now. Mummy's dead and gone, so you don't have to worry about her any-more, and neither does he. He is no longer taking his vitamins and never will again."

"How d'you know that?"

"I know for sure he won't. He values you too much. And anyway, the things that were driving his behaviour are gone now, Mummy's gone, Jarrod's gone, the church will benefit from these changes alone. You do realize that you're what kept that place up and running in one piece all this time."

"I did?" Alberta had never thought about it like that. "I only did what had to be done."

"And sometimes more. So brace yourself and say yes, for goodness sake. I have to go now."

Molly's energy faded in a slight draft.

Alberta shivered and roused herself from what seemed to be a strange state of almost dreaming. Her cocoa had gone cold and she wondered why. "That is so strange," she muttered. She looked at the mantle clock with the Westminster chime. Why didn't I even hear that? Where did the last two hours go? It should have chimed at least eight times. Was that Daddy I was talking to? It couldn't have been.

Her mind wandered back to the church and the day that had just passed, then on to Pastor Teddy and to their childhood. Teddy was always so prissy, even when we were in kindergarten. The other boys used to make such fun of him. I went to bat for him once and was so razzed by the other kids that I never did it again. I always thought there was something sweet and vulnerable about him, though I couldn't let on. Even in high school. He never went to the dances. I always went alone. Of course, except for Linda and Robbie, no one had a boyfriend. Her thoughts wandered on across the years of their shared childhood. He was always so kind. I often wondered how he could be like that with Aggie being such an ogre.

Alberta drained her mug of the cocoa. Goodness, this is cold. How long have I been sitting here? She looked at her watch, then looked at it again. It's eleven o'clock already.

Morning came too early for Alberta. She was jarred

out of sleep by the din of her alarm clock. She hit the button to silence it, then turned onto her back. "Oh," she groaned, "I don't want to get up. I don't want to get dressed. I don't want to have breakfast, and I especially don't want to go to work this morning." She rubbed her eyes into wakefulness. Her stomach griped. "Well, maybe I'd like breakfast." She rolled out of bed and stuck her feet into her slippers. I'd love to stay home today, she thought. I've about had enough of that place, at least until Jarrod vacates.

She dawdled over breakfast and dressing. Her thoughts turned to Teddy again. I'm still not convinced that Teddy's recovery is solid. I don't want to deal with that kind of problem. I wish Daddy was really here. She took her coffee over to her father's recliner and hunkered down into the coziness of it. I wonder what Daddy would say. She imagined talking to her father as she used to when he was alive. She nestled into the chair and closed her eyes. In her mind her father's rough features became clear and it was as if he was there talking to her. She could see his lips moving and strained to hear what he was saying.

"Daddy, what should I do?" Her brow wrinkled in her distress. "You've known Teddy as long as I have. You know what he's about. Can I trust him to be free of alcohol and Aggie's influence?" Her breathing deepened and she slipped into a dream of her father. It was as if they were meeting in a conference room. Her father sat at the head of the table and spoke.

"Bertie, you know already what to do." Her father patted her hand. "You know that Teddy is a good and trustworthy person. That it was Aggie's influence that drove him to drink." He tented his hands and looked over the top of them at her. "Marry Teddy. You'll have good companionship for the rest of your lives."

"Was that you last evening?"

Her father shook his head. "A friend of mine. You should heed what she said; she knows."

Alberta's head jerked forward and she woke. "You were so close, Daddy." She closed her eyes again to try to recapture the image and presence of her father. She reviewed what her father had said. The tone and warmth of his message was all that was left. Alberta sighed. I still miss you, Daddy.

"I'm sorry I was not here this morning, Pastor Teddy. After the meeting last evening I was very tired and didn't sleep well." Alberta dropped her purse into the left bottom drawer of her desk.

"Think nothing of it, Miss Alberta." Teddy smiled down at her. "I really didn't expect to see you at all today."

"Oh, I couldn't do that," said Alberta. "I've never been away for any reason except vacation these last thirty years. Why, I haven't even taken sick days."

"Sh-sh," said Teddy. "I know you haven't. You've been very reliable." He patted her hand. "Don't fret over it."

Alberta drew a deep breath and let it out in a gusty sigh. "You're right. I'm being a perfectionist." She collected up some pencils and began to sharpen them.

"Has Jarrod vacated yet?"

"His office is cleaned out and there's no sign of him." Teddy sniffed. "We're well clear of him."

"He must have come during the night," said Alberta. "He even left his key," said Teddy.

Alberta left work early. She wiped her damp boots on the mat at her front door.

"Miss Alberta, Miss Alberta." The call came from near at hand. It was Mrs. Winters from next door. She scuffled up the path to Alberta's door. "I was worried about you. I saw your lights on half the night and I wondered. Especially when I saw a man coming to the front door early this morning. He got in too. He was there one minute, then I blinked and he was gone. He bore a remarkable resemblance to your dear departed Daddy." She paused for breath.

"I'm fine," said Alberta. "I had a late meeting last evening and I fell asleep in the armchair while I was drinking my hot chocolate." She arched her grey eyebrows over the frame of her glasses. "As for the man at my door, I don't know what or who you saw, but I certainly didn't let any strangers into my house in the dead of night." Alberta pushed the key into the lock. "Thank you for taking such good care of me."

"Come over and have tea with me sometime."

I must call Jane. Alberta began to think of the strange events of last evening again. Darn, I can't call Jane. It's my problem and I have to deal wit it. She hung her coat on the rack and slipped out of her boots. She walked stocking-footed into the kitchen and put the kettle on for tea. Why am I viewing this as a problem? she wondered. It shouldn't be a problem. I need to talk to Jane.

The kettle whistled and Alberta put down the tea to steep. Presently the door bell rang.

"Hello, Danny. You're working for the flower industry. I'd heard you went to agricultural college, but it doesn't seem that long ago."

"Long enough, Miss Alberta. These are for you."

Danny handed her a large basket of flowers.

"Why Danny, you shouldn't have."

"I didn't." Danny coloured slightly.

"D'you know who did?" Alberta sniffed the roses. Their sweet scent brought back the memory of her mother's garden.

"No, uh uh, the order came by phone and was paid with a credit card that I don't have access to yet."

"And they really are for me?" Alberta sniffed the flowers once more.

"You could always read the card," said Danny.

"Of course. My mind is distracted today. Will you come in for some tea?"

"No thanks, Miss Alberta, I have several more stops to make before quitting time." Danny turned to go. "Nice seeing you, Miss Alberta." He turned to wave but the door was already closing.

Alberta carried the bouquet to the kitchen. Who in the world would send me flowers? she thought. She set the bouquet by the sink and rummaged carefully among the leaves to find the card. She stood looking at the card, savouring the unusual and unexpected gift. Presently she opened the envelope. It was from Teddy. "Oh," said Alberta, "Oh. Teddy dear, you shouldn't have. These must have cost a mint. I'll have to put them in something special." She went to the dining room where her mother's crystal was stored and took out the tallest cut glass vase and carried it out to the kitchen.

"There," she said. "That's just lovely." She set the bouquet in the centre of the kitchen table then stood back to admire it. "That was so thoughtful of dear Teddy." This time she heard herself address Teddy as dear. "Oh, no, this complicates things. I do really need to talk to Jane."

Chapter 15

Alberta opened her front door to Teddy's knock that evening. He stood there and regarded her with warmth in his eyes. He held an enormous box of Swiss chocolates in his hands. He blushed and ducked his head. "May I come in, Miss Alberta? I think we have much to discuss."

Alberta opened the door wider and stood aside to allow Teddy entrance. She turned and led the way toward the coziness of the kitchen.

Teddy closed the door behind himself, took off his coat and hung it neatly on the hall tree. He followed Alberta to the kitchen. There was a somewhat awkward silence between them.

"Sit in then,Teddy and I'll make us a cup of tea." Alberta finally managed a slight smile. "I made a tray of brownies after work to go with our morning coffee tomorrow, but we can have some now if you like."

Teddy nodded and watched Alberta as she moved around the kitchen.

"Stop staring, please Teddy. You're making me nervous." She filled the kettle and plugged it in to come to a boil, then began to slice generous pieces of brownie still a little warm from the oven. "D'you want some squirt on it?"

"Yes please." Teddy held out his plate. "Whoever invented pressurized cream in a can did the world a great service."

"Indeed they did." Alberta served herself and pulled her chair in to the table. The kettle came to a boil and Alberta rose to put the tea down to steep. "That'll be ready to drink in a few minutes." She sat down again. She sat regarding Teddy across the table then said: "Yes, I think we should talk. We need to." She cleared her throat. "I'm sorry, I'm feeling a little nervous. Did you really mean what you said about us getting married?"

"Yes, yes I did," said Teddy. "I would have asked you sooner and under better circumstances than in front of everyone in the middle of a disagreement with Jarrod."

Alberta chuckled. "Yes, that was not the best time,

but it certainly shut Jarrod up."

"And shocked a lot of people." Teddy managed a crooked smile that did not quite take. "I should have done it sooner with just you and me, not half the church."

"People were not as shocked as you think. Several of them said it was about time."

"But what if you had wanted to say no?" Teddy sat still waiting for her answer. "I didn't give you much choice in the matter. You know, I wanted to ask you long ago but I didn't dare."

Alberta stared at her half eaten brownie then glanced up at Teddy. "Why didn't you?"

Teddy sighed. "Mummy. She would have made our lives a misery each in our own way and I wouldn't put you or me through that."

"Thank you for that, Teddy. If we had to consider her too, I probably would have said no."

"So you're saying yes?" Teddy's eyes lighted up in hope.

"Yes, I'm saying yes."

"I'm so glad," said Teddy.

"I saw the way she treated you in public and she was very rude to me and the other staff besides. I thought if she was that bad at church how was she at home?"

"Worse," said Teddy. "The only person she tolerated was Jarrod. But she's gone now and so is Jarrod, and I'm glad. A terrible thing to say, but I'm glad."

They finished their dessert in silence. Teddy scraped up the last of his crumbs then said: "Shall we look for rings tomorrow and set a date? I'm sure there are a lot of things to agree on and to organize to plan a wedding."

The next day Teddy took Alberta shopping. They picked out an old-fashioned setting resembling an Apothecary rose and two plain bands that matched.

"I have a friend in the ministry who can marry us. I won't be able to do the ceremony myself. I'll see when he's available."

"I've been thinking," said Alberta. "Why don't we

have a chapel service and just invite our closest friends, and later have a big wedding celebration where we invite the whole congregation, whoever can come? We don't need gifts. I'm sure we've got two very well stocked households."

"What about a date?" asked Teddy

"How about a May wedding? Easter will be over, and church activities will have quieted down by then. Besides my birthday is May 6th, and it falls on a Saturday this year."

"Perfect!" said Teddy, "I wouldn't have thought of that." He took Alberta's hand. "What about a honeymoon? Is there somewhere you'd like to go?"

"I've always wanted to do that Rocky Mountain train trip to British Columbia. We could get one of those little roomettes for ourselves."

"Excellent idea, I wouldn't have thought of that either. It'll take us a week or so. I'll have to get someone to cover for me while I'm gone. What about you?"

"We'll probably have at least an interim by then.

He or she could fill in for you. There won't be very much going on at church just then, so that person could handle all the affairs until we come back," said Alberta. "You'll have to get on that right away. Jane can be the go to person if anything comes up."

"When are we going to announce our plans?" asked Teddy. "If we're only having a small gathering we'd better not announce anything until we're ready to leave."

"I'll have to tell Jane. She's my best friend, and I want her at the ceremony. And of course, your minister friend will have to know. Other than that, I don't think we need to make an announcement until the Sunday before departure. Jane can handle the rest. She's got a good head and she's safe as banks with a confidence."

"So it's settled then. We'll just elope."

It was a reunion between old friends and colleagues when Teddy introduced Alberta to his good friend Dave. They had been students together in seminary, so old times were recalled and all the pranks and mishaps they had been up to. Over the years they had gradually lost touch with each other so there was a lot to talk about. Dave was delighted to perform the ceremony. Jane and Sam were in attendance and no one at the church knew about it until after they returned home. Teddy asked Dave's son to videotape the ceremony so that they could share it with the congregation at their reception later. Soon it was time to leave. Goodbyes were said, and everyone came to wave then off as they left for the train station.

Their trip through the Rockies was filled with the stunning and magnificent views that passed their windows as the train trundled its way through the forests and past the green blue waters of the streams and lakes of the mountains. Teddy videotaped their trip all through the daylight hours and lamented the thick darkness that fell after sunset.

"I think, if you could, you'd tape the whole trip from start to finish," said Alberta. She laughed. "Are you going to submit it as a travelogue to the railway?"

"I should," said Teddy. "It never occurred to me. I just want our friends in the congregation to enjoy it as much as I do."

"As much as we do," said Alberta. "And it'll be over too soon."

"At least we'll have the video for ourselves," said Teddy. He hoisted the camera to viewing height once more.

As soon as they returned, the news of their nuptials spread like a grass fire, and those who hadn't already heard it off the grapevine were taken by surprise when Teddy introduced Alberta as his wife from the pulpit the first Sunday they were home. The whole congregation broke out in cheers. A few people were envious, and others chose to be insulted that they weren't invited.

"Everyone is invited to our reception next Saturday. I had my friend's son videotape the whole ceremony so no one would feel left out. We just wanted a simple, private ceremony so we went to Pastor Dave, who's a friend from seminary days."

Saturday was a sunny day, perfect for a reception. The grass carried the fresh green of springtime, and the trees were leafing out almost to their full summer garb. The birds were singing their hearts out to their mates, and Teddy and Alberta were kept busy making arrangements for their afternoon reception.

"D'you think we should have had a wedding cake?" asked Alberta. "It seems a little extravagant for our age and the fact that we eloped."

Teddy set down the stack of napkins he was arranging on the table. "Why didn't I think of that? Of course we should have had a wedding cake. That's important to a bride. I'm just sorry I didn't think of it in time." Teddy looked very downcast at his lack of foresight.

"It's alright, Teddy, it's not that important." Alberta opened the guest book and set it on the little table by the door. She had carried the table from the Ladies' Parlour when they had first come in and now set the open guest book she had bought for the occasion on it.

The outside door banged open, and Jane and Sam carried in a large, decorated wedding cake on a tray. "I never heard you say what you were going to do about a wedding cake so I took the liberty," said Jane. "I was lucky. The bakery had a cancellation yesterday, but by the time it came, the cake had already gone into the oven. I talked Linda at the bakery into decorating it anyway and said I'd buy it."

"Oh, bless you, Jane. Neither Teddy nor I thought of it until just now. Set it in the middle of the long table." Alberta went over to inspect the cake.

"D'you like it?" asked Jane.

"It's a beautiful cake," said Alberta.

"It's perfect," said Teddy.

"You don't think it's too ornate? I had to slow Linda down when she found out who it was for. She was all set to add more velvet ribbons and roses until I stopped her."

"A rose or two less and it would have been too plain,"

said Alberta. "It's perfect." She gave Jane a hug. "Thank you so much."

"What's left to do?" asked Sam.

"Just set up a few small tables around the room and some of those folding chairs," said Teddy. "I had the janitor bring them up from downstairs last evening."

"By the way," said Jane, "Sam and I have set a date for our wedding."

"Excellent," said Teddy. "I hope you want me to perform the ceremony?"

"Of course we do. You're our favourite pastor," said Jane.

"When's the day?" asked Alberta.

"September 4th," said Jane. "In the morning."

"We've decided on a fall theme," said Sam. "The kids will be back in school the next Monday and they won't be into their fall activities yet, so the parents will be able to come."

"If we have it in the morning they'll have the rest of the day to do what they usually do on the last Saturday afternoon of the summer," said Jane.

"We have a lot of friends and family who have young children," said Sam.

"Good thinking," said Teddy. He began fanning the dessert forks into arrangements next to the cake. "There, I think that looks nice, don't you Alberta?"

"Lovely, Teddy. Perhaps some napkins to go with it."

The outside door rattled and swung open again and several of the ladies from the sewing circle came in bearing large trays of sandwiches.

"My goodness," said Alberta. "I didn't know you were going to do all that."

"It was a surprise." Lydia set her tray down on the table. "We have several more yet. Everyone was eager to contribute."

"We thank you very much." Alberta sniffed back an errant tear.

"I don't know who organized it but we're certainly grateful," said Teddy.

"It was Jane's idea," said Diane. "She thought that

we should do something to help you celebrate. After all, it's not often our pastor gets married."

The outside door banged again, and Mary came into the hall carrying the huge punch bowl and ladle. "I have paper cups in the car still, if someone will get them for me, please. I took this home after church to wash. I'm glad I did. It was pretty dusty." She set the bowl and ladle on the table. "Martha and Liz are bringing the juice to make the punch"

Preparations continued apace with lots of laughter and a few "oops, I didn't mean to do that," and many thank you's and excuse me's. About two o'clock the congregation started arriving and the wedding film started rolling. Most of the people were there, many carrying wrapped gifts. It was a happy occasion. After the cake was cut and served, someone offered a toast. Then Teddy hushed everyone and gave an announcement of his own. "On September 4th, Jane Ridgeway and Pastor Sam are going to tie the knot too. We look forward to their nuptials as well." This was followed by applause and handshakes.

"Are you going to open gifts soon?" asked Barbara Ann. "I love seeing presents opened and I want to see what everybody brought. Besides, I said I'd clean up the kitchen."

Later that evening Teddy propped his stockinged feet on the hassock and said: "I'd say we've had a pretty successful start to the year. The ladies' strike is over, and everything ended with accomplishing their aim. Jarrod's gone, and so are his grandiose plans for pageants. I'll never have to swing from the ceiling again."

"No one else will either," said Alberta.

"Peace is currently reigning in our little congregation."

"Long may it continue." Alberta settled herself into her father's chair with the last cup of the supper tea.

"That was a fine thing the congregation did for us."

"I think that was mostly Jane's doing. She's good at organizing and getting people on board to do things. I think she may have been behind the ladies' strike though she never said anything."

"Why weren't you involved?"

"I couldn't be. Someone had to keep the day to day running of the place up." Alberta set her now empty cup on the side table. "Besides, the less I knew, the better."

Teddy sighed. "I certainly wasn't any help. I couldn't even stand up to my own mother."

"Water under the bridge," said Alberta.